MW01172960

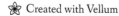 Created with Vellum

Christmas
on
King Street

a novella

ASHLEY CLARK

CONTENTS

ONE

TWINKLE LIGHTS ARE PERFECTLY INTERTWINED with fresh green garland, and the smell of a cinnamon candle wafts toward me from inside this dress shop on King Street.

The setting is Christmasy perfection.

Yet nothing in my life is going according to plan.

This is why I like flowers so much. You choose a seed, you plant that seed, and with a little water and sunshine, a flower will shimmy its way through the ground.

Maybe the problem is that fewer flowers bloom in the winter. Maybe it's because I'm worried whether I'll still run my New Orleans flower shop, The Prickly Rose, come spring.

Or *maybe* it's because the plans I had for my life seem to have been suddenly and unceremoniously covered with too much topsoil.

Okay, so the analogy kind of broke down there, but you see what I mean.

Whatever the case, when my boyfriend Sullivan wanted to come home to Charleston for Christmas and that meant seeing my best friend Harper, I jumped in his Jeep so fast you would've thought I was filming some kind of ridiculous Instagram reel. You know the ones, where people will stop at nothing for a literal five seconds of fame.

Y'all, I was embarrassing myself long before the days of Instagram.

So that's how I got here... standing inside Harper's store on King Street—adorably named Second Story—and unloading a box of vintage items my mom asked me to haul all the way here from New Orleans.

And I use the term "vintage" very loosely. Let's just say I'm going to need some Claritin after the amount of dust I'm inhaling.

"Why do you have that look on your face?" Harper's bracelets jangle as she reaches to remove one of my earbuds. She is the only person I would let do this without consequence, Sullivan included. Somehow, Harper is just too... nice... for anyone to get mad at her. "Are you listening to Coldplay again?"

The truth is, I *am* listening to Coldplay, and the fact she knows the effect their music has on my mood is either a testament to my need for some new playlists or proof of how well she knows me. Maybe both.

She takes my hesitation as confirmation, handing back my earbud and picking up the box of dusty knick knacks to move them. Apparently she wants to have the forthcoming conversation with nothing in the way.

"Alice?" She draws out my name. "It's Christmastime. What is with you and the moody music?"

I raise my chin, knowing full well I have little argument to make here but deciding to try anyway. "Coldplay is hardly *moody music*, thank you."

Harper raises one eyebrow.

I try a different approach. "Musical genres are all relative if you think about it. It's not like I'm listening to emo or something."

Her eyes widen.

"What?" I ask.

"Oh nothing—it's just been a really long time since I've heard anyone use the term *emo*."

I smirk at this, shaking my head. "Great, so now I'm both moody and out of date."

"See, now you're getting it," she teases. I laugh, knowing full well her teasing is good spirited. And maybe with just the teeniest bit of truth.

"Alice, you've been here a full twenty-four hours and have yet to tell me what's going on. I'm not fooled by the fake smile you've been putting on all afternoon while the store was open." Harper hesitates. "Thanks for helping me with the store, by the way. You didn't have to do that."

"I was happy to help." *It gets my mind off other matters...* I start to say, then catch myself.

"Where is your sparkle?" She asks the question directly, as though I should have known I sparkled to begin with and further know where my glitter has gone.

I consider my response. "The last couple of years have been... hard."

Harper nods knowingly. And though she has everything I want—a husband and a store—I also know she understands. She almost lost someone very dear to her when they got sick this time last year.

"Business or personal?"

I take a deep breath. Might as well get it all out. "Both?" I admit with an honesty that surprises even myself. "I mean... I love Sullivan. And I know he loves me too. But it's been two years since we started dating, and I'm really feeling the pressure of wanting to know what's next for us."

"Have you talked with him about it?"

I shrug. "Sort of." Trailing my finger along the table where the box of old items sat moments prior, I absentmind-edly trace snowflake shapes against the wood. "He just assures me he's committed and wants to take the next steps when the timing is right."

Harper puckers her bottom lip, her signature expression when considering something. "I guess that seems reasonable enough."

"Reasonable and exciting are two different things."

"Indeed." She gives my arm a sympathy squeeze. "And The Prickly Rose? What about that?"

This question pangs my heart, and I suck in a deep breath as though I've been lightly stabbed—is light stabbing a thing? You know, like a throbbing cut only it's not deep enough for anyone to rush to your rescue...

"Let's just say the wedding business isn't exactly buzzing when there's a global pandemic."

"But you sell flowers for other events and occasions... and you have your subscription boxes."

"By the grace of God, yes." I tap my fingers rhythmi-cally now, trying to find a rhyme or reason for all of this. "Without the subscription boxes and bouquets, there is no way the business would have made it. But even still..." I shake my head. "We offer a unique type of bouquet service. It's just..."

"Been hard." Harper finishes.

I nod once more. "How have you managed to keep Second Story afloat?"

"We've moved a lot of our business online, especially to social media. Plus... Millie. My grandmother-in-law meets no strangers. And in our case, that means everyone is a potential customer."

I laugh. That does sound like Millie.

"Alice?"

I bite my lip gently, nervous for what she might say. "Yes?"

"You said it's been hard. *How* hard?"

I tug at the hem of my strawberry-printed cardigan. "I-may-have-to-shut-down-next-month hard."

Now she understands. Surprise, then empathy, pass over her expression in that order as the taut lines on her forehead loosen. "Can I help?"

I shake my head. "If only you could. It would honestly take a Christmas miracle at this point."

"What about your aunt? It was her store before you teamed up together, right? Can she do something?"

"Honestly, my aunt is ready to close the doors. She's been saying for months that it was nice while it lasted, but we can't keep losing all the money we worked for. If we sell The Prickly Rose now, we can probably walk away with a substantial nest egg for our next project, but if we let the business bottom out..."

"Then it could be a different story?"

Quiet tears begin to stream from my eyes. Then they are joined by many more.

"Harper, what am I going to do?" I ask the question as though she may have the answer.

She meets my gaze with hope in her eyes. "I don't know... but I *do* know you will figure it out. There's a next thing for you, Alice, just like there was for me when Millie and I started our dress shop here on King Street. Sometimes our *next* arrives wearing vintage shoes, is all."

I smile at her analogy—how very Harper of her and yet

how fittingly kind. Then I wipe the tears from my eyes and step over to the place she set the box.

"Enough wallowing. Let me know where to put this stuff."

Harper grins, following my lead. "That really depends on what you find in there. Clothes and shoes will need to be cleaned thoroughly and inspected. Knick knacks can go in a separate pile. And if you find anything you think may be valuable, separate it from the rest so we can track down the story behind it."

I make a mental note of this. I do love a good story.

"I'm going to close out the register while you work." Harper turns to go.

"Sounds good," I say over my shoulder as she steps behind me toward the register.

I reach toward a scarf on a nearby display and wrap it over my face several times, using it as a mask to protect my nose from dust. Harper laughs at my antics from several feet away, but several puffs of dust float upward as I begin rifling through the items, proving what a smart idea my scarf-mask really is.

The items in the box are unassuming at best. Some clothes well past their prime. A stack of books that are old enough to be aged but young enough to fetch little in the way of resale prices on the Internet.

I continue removing items from the box, growing increasingly less optimistic that I'll find treasure by the moment.

And then I get to the bottom of the pile, and I see it.

A vintage music box, with a Christmas tree hand-painted on the top. I blow off the dust, then gingerly wind and open the box to reveal an ice-skating figurine inside.

The piece is absolutely stunning, but as the music

begins to play, it's not the painting or the figurine that arrests my attention.

It's the song.

Melodic and almost haunting, the jazzy music envelops me.

See, I am a trained vocalist and know the classical numbers. This particular song is not one of those. An original composition for the music box, perhaps?

And yet in the song are flashes of my childhood. Popsicle summers and new-sweater winters. Movies curled up beside my mother on the sofa.

I've heard this song before. My mother used to sing it to me all the time. This song is the reason I began loving jazz. From the arms of my mother, my interest was born.

In an unexpected way, I feel as though the music box owner and I share a history through this song, and I'm suddenly invested in learning more.

Why was the music box bundled up with all these discarded items? Did my mother even know she'd placed it there?

"Alice?" Harper asks. She must have noticed my hesitation because she comes to stand beside me. "Wow, that box is beautiful. See, I told you that you never know when you'll find a hidden gem."

I glance up at her quizzically. "Is there any chance this item was added to the box I brought?"

She shakes her head. "No, I don't think so. I'm fairly sure everything in there came straight from your mother."

My hope plummets, though I'm not altogether sure for what I was hoping.

Harper takes the box from my hands and looks it over. "Well, let me ask this. Why are you intent on finding out?"

Why *was* I intent on finding out? This was a good question.

"I just want to learn more about the music box." The words come out as a question rather than a statement.

Harper begins to grin as though she isn't buying my answer. "Alice, what are you planning?"

She knows me far too well.

Still, I'm about to say I'm not planning anything, when a tiny card inside the music box catches my eye...

TWO

SULLIVAN SLID a Nespresso pod into his buddy Peter's machine and closed his eyes as the coffee whirred into existence.

Technically, the machine belonged to Peter's wife Harper and his grandmother Millie—Peter didn't drink coffee despite their collective attempts to convert him.

Sullivan took a deep breath as a tidy fountain of coffee poured into his mug.

Last night marked another notch in a long streak of sleepless evenings. He had so much on his mind, yet he didn't know who besides the Lord he could talk to. He'd been asking God for clarity, and that was part of the problem... God had begun giving it.

But Sullivan wanted to sort through all the answers before approaching Alice. She was his serious girlfriend, for crying out loud. She didn't need the responsibility of interpreting his emotions. He just wasn't going to put that on her.

And so meanwhile, his emotions remained... well, unsorted.

When Aunt Beth invited he and Alice for Christmas, the opportunity to come home to Charleston seemed a perfectly-timed distraction.

And yet, it seemed the heaviness of his heart had followed him home.

Sullivan took the first steamy sip from his coffee as Peter worked a glass windowpane through the doorway. "You want some help, man?" Sullivan asked, setting his mug down.

"No, I've got it, but thanks." Peter gently leaned the glass panes against the kitchen cabinets, wiping sweat from his forehead.

"Should I ask what that is?" Sullivan had gotten used to Peter's treasure hunting and had even participated in the endeavors more than once. In fact, he liked to take credit for helping Peter discover the furniture that led Peter to his long-lost grandmother... the spunky Millie whom they all loved.

"Leaded glass."

"Of course." Sullivan took another drink of his coffee.

"I salvaged it from a two-hundred-year-old house. There's more in the truck." Peter raised his eyebrows in excitement.

Sullivan laughed. He had to appreciate his buddy's interest in preserving history and artifacts.

"You're having another coffee?" Peter asked. "That's got to be the fourth one today." He glanced at the watch on his wrist. "And it's only three o'clock."

"Okay, okay." Sullivan held up his free hand. "No need to coffee-shame me, man—I'll 'fess up. I didn't sleep well last night."

"That's what you said yesterday."

Sullivan hesitated.

"You do realize I'm not going to let you off the hook until you tell me what's going on?"

Yes, Sullivan had a hunch this conversation would head in that direction. And yet... ugh, he did not want to talk about it.

Peter sat at the table and motioned for Sullivan to do the same, tossing him a coaster. "Better to get it out now before Millie shows up and the whole city knows."

Sullivan relished the warmth of the mug between his hands. "Obviously I went back to medical school and then started my residency last year. In the middle of the pandemic."

With his elbow on the table, Peter rested his chin on his fist. "Yeah, you don't talk about that much."

"I..." Sullivan hesitated, trying to find the right words. He was known as a fun-loving guy, and though he didn't mind talking about *other* people's feelings... Alice's, for example... plumbing his own emotions felt like walking through a minefield with a wish and a prayer.

He sighed. Maybe there were no words. "It was really bad, Peter... the things I saw. And I know God put me there for that time and place, to make a difference in the midst of such hopelessness and pain. I don't regret it. I *did* make a difference. But now..."

Sullivan rubbed his open palm with his thumb. "Now the desire to stay there and complete my residency... well, it's gone." He looked up at his buddy. "If I'm being honest."

Peter's eyes widened. "No wonder it was a four-coffee-kind-of-day."

"You're telling me."

"Are you sure you're not just weary? Burned-out and needing a break?"

Sullivan considered this. "I've been asking myself that

question for months now, because in some ways burn-out would actually be easier. But no." He shook his head. "I'm not cut out for it long term."

"So what are you going to do next?"

Sullivan blew out a deep breath very slowly. "That is the million dollar question."

"What does Alice think?" Peter tossed a glance toward the window pane resting against the cabinets, probably making sure it wasn't sliding.

"I haven't told her."

Peter's gaze snapped back to Sullivan. "Why are you telling *me* before Alice?"

Sullivan buried his face in his hands. "Ugh, dude, I know. I have to talk to her."

"No kidding."

"It's just..." Sullivan's words drifted off. "She wants to get *married*, Peter. Married."

"You've been dating two years. Of course she wants to get married. Do you have something against the institution? Because I, for one, am highly in favor of it."

"Okay, enough of your newlywed-ish gushing. Of course I want to get married. *To Alice.* The problem is, I no longer have a plan for the future. Don't you see?"

Peter scratched his head. "So let me get this straight. You're not telling Alice about a major life decision that affects you both because you think you need to have the decision made on your own first?"

"Not exactly how I would word it, but yes." Sullivan breathed in the welcome aroma of his coffee before taking a longer sip. "She needs to know what I'm proposing. I can't promise my life to her and only offer question marks and baggage."

Peter groaned. "Come on. We both know you offer far

more than that... you also have a really large collection of vinyl albums."

Sullivan smirked. "I'm serious, man." He shook his head. "I need to figure this stuff out—get a plan going—before I talk to her. She deserves to know what I have ahead of me."

Peter sat quietly, looking at his friend.

"What are you not saying?" Sullivan had a suspicion he already knew the answer.

"Just that maybe Alice would like to figure that out *with* you. Maybe you should give her a little more credit."

"Maybe." But Sullivan's pride was not going to let him find out. "Look, all I need to do is get my head on straight and gain some clarity. Maybe even find another job first. Then I'll talk to Alice, okay? So you needn't worry that you're in some cone of confidence."

"Good, because I'm bad with secrets."

Sullivan already knew that much. Peter had the worst poker face of everyone he knew.

Peter stood, patting his friend on the shoulder. "You'll figure it out, man. You always do."

"I appreciate that." If only he could be as sure as he sounded.

Not long after their coffee break, Sullivan's girlfriend Alice and Peter's wife Harper burst through the door in a fit of laughter.

It was good seeing Alice like this. Sullivan hadn't heard her laugh so freely in a long time. Something he hadn't realized until now.

Of course he knew the financial woes of Alice's flower

shop were taking a toll on her. He admired her ability to maintain a clear head despite it all and wasn't sure he'd be able to do the same if the situation were reversed.

Alice loved that shop. She and her aunt had poured so much into it for years. The prospect of having to make an unplanned career change? Not exactly comfortable.

And yet, even still... he wondered now if there was more to Alice's discontent than just the store, and if maybe his attitude of twirling his thumbs about the topic of marriage had weighed down on her.

Maybe Peter was right. Maybe he should talk to her and admit that all his own plans seemed to be falling apart.

Alice, his commitment to his faith, and his love of old jazz were about the *only* three things Sullivan was sure of these days.

Regardless, now was not the time for soul searching.

Alice flipped her fiery curls over her shoulder as she shut the front door behind herself and Harper, then approached where Sullivan and Peter now sat in the living room.

She took Sullivan's breath away. It may sound cliche, but every time he looked at her after they'd been apart, his breath caught in his chest. She would never *not* be the love of his life.

He stepped over to her, gently putting one hand on her back and giving her a kiss he wished could've lasted longer.

She bit down on her bottom lip as she pulled away, a twinkle in her eyes. No matter the reason, it was *so good* to see that twinkle back in her eyes. "You're never going to believe what we found today."

Sullivan crossed his arms and grinned. Between this and Peter's leaded glass, he was surrounded by people who loved old stuff. Not that he didn't appreciate history himself, but when Peter and Harper were around there was no telling what they were going to salvage.

"Something from Second Story, I take it?"

Alice nodded twice, her excitement palpable. She reached into the bag she carried and carefully slid a music box out.

"Wow. That's... really old."

"Cool, right?" She was practically glowing and cradled the music box as though it were a strand of priceless jewels. "I'm going to track down the history!"

Sullivan opened his mouth to speak, then thought better of it and stopped himself. Nothing he was thinking would be helpful in this moment.

Peter stepped closer. "Looks like a ratchet winding device, which would date it in approximately the twentieth century."

Sullivan turned to his buddy, shaking his head in disbelief. "You never cease to surprise me. How would you possibly know that?"

Peter shrugged, laughing. "Around here, I find a surprising number of artifacts from that time period. The city is very historic."

Sullivan shared a humored smile with Alice. She slid the music box back into the protective bag she'd carried it in, then gently set the whole thing down on the coffee table at the center of the room. Knowing Peter, the table was probably made out of reclaimed wood from some ancient house or shipwreck.

The four of them settled in on the loveseat and couch, and Sullivan draped his arm over Alice's shoulders. She fit perfectly there. From this vantage point he could breathe in the smell of her hair—the fragrance of all kinds of flowers.

"So, is the owner of the music box different from whoever gave to Second Story?" he asked.

Alice stilled. "You could say that..."

He cringed inside. He really hoped this search wouldn't turn up to be another disappointment for Alice. How much more could her heart take?

Sullivan tried taking a different angle. "What are you going to do when you find him or her?"

"I'm not *exactly* sure about that either." With one finger, she hooked her beautiful hair behind her ears.

He looked into her eyes—trying to tell her with his gaze that he *saw* her, despite the others in the room—and her lips quirked into a half-grin. "I'm sure you'll figure out all the details. Sometimes the search is half the fun."

"Thank you." Her words were sweet, and he wanted to kiss her again. "How was your day?" she asked.

"Let's just say it involved helping Peter with a whole heap of leaded glass."

Alice chuckled.

But Harper sat up straighter. "Peter!" she chided. "I thought we agreed no more window panes after last time."

He clenched his teeth and held up his hands. "Would it help if I said these are from the Reconstruction Era and that they'll sell for a lot?"

She pinched her fingers together. "That helps just a tiny bit."

Peter laughed, pulling her closer, and Harper responded by falling into his hug and returning his laughter.

Sullivan's heart tugged, seeing his friends so happy. He wanted to be married to Alice. He *really* wanted to be married to Alice.

He just needed to figure out the rest of the plan and what he had to offer.

THREE

I CAN'T SLIP A WINK, and Harper's instance our whole group of friends watch *It's a Wonderful Life* tonight is only partially to blame.

Even Peter's grandmother Millie got in on the fun earlier, telling us she saw *It's a Wonderful Life* in the theater when it came out, which is really mind-boggling when you think about it.

But every time I try to sleep, I hear the refrain of that song in the music box... almost like it's calling me, over and over again. I spent some time in prayer then did deep breathing exercises, and while both things helped my anxiety, neither helped me sleep.

So here I am. Staring at the music box on my nightstand as the first rays of dawn peek through my window. I'm in the process of debating how early is too early to call my mother back in New Orleans when I remember today is the day she teaches music lessons to kids before school starts.

Perfect.

I stand from the bed, not bothering with my messy hair but belting my robe over my pajamas, and then I tiptoe through the house with the music box in my hands and my phone in my robe pocket.

Opening the door to the back porch will be tricky because it creaks sometimes, but I'm confident I can get it open without waking anyone.

The whole scene makes me feel a bit like a thief in the night—well, early dawn, but you get the picture—and I laugh quietly to myself even as a gust of cool air greets me from outside.

I'll have to make this call quick so I don't catch a chill, but I don't want to risk waking anyone in the house. I can tell the whole of them already think I'm off on a wild goose chase with this music box.

And maybe I am. But maybe it's a wild goose chase I really need right now.

Closing the door behind me, I cozy onto the patio furniture and slip a blanket over my legs.

Then I dial my mother's number on my phone. Amazing to think that a few short years ago, I didn't even know if she was alive.

God has restored so much in that time. Of course I would rather that it wasn't broken in the first place, but that's the way life is sometimes, right?

The phone rings several times before she answers. "Alice? Everything all right?"

Clearly I don't have a reputation for getting up this early.

"Yes, I'm fine." I resituate my feet under the blanket for more warmth. My gaze goes to the music box I've carried outside. "I just couldn't sleep."

"That's very unlike you. Are you sure you're fine?"

"Well... fine-ish." I hesitate. "Mom, do you remember

that song you used to sing when I was a little girl?" I proceed to hum the tune.

"Of course. My mother used to sing it to your aunt and I when we were kids. Well, I was a kid... your aunt was a lot older than me, so she was a teenager at that time."

"Do you know where Grandma first heard the song?" I trail my finger along the beautiful, painted top of the music box. I can't believe it was almost discarded. Lost...

My mother sighs.

"What are you not telling me?"

"It's kind of a sad story, which is why I only sang you the song and never told you this part... but my mother always used to say that the song was a gift from a family friend."

I frown. "A gift?" But why would that be sad?

"He fought during World War II and didn't return. She never really knew him."

"How would the song be from him then?" I am trying to put the pieces together, but it doesn't make much sense. And why would my own mother think the song worth passing down like a treasure? Doesn't that indicate importance?

"The story goes that after the war, my grandmother opened the front door and found the box with a note inside saying the gift was for my mother."

"A gift?"

"Yes. A music box that played the song."

My breath hitches. She does not seem to realize she's given away that very box.

The same box I am holding now. The same *history* I am holding now.

"Mom, did that part of your family have any connection to Charleston?"

"Oh, yes. They lived there a good while before settling in New Orleans. I guess the music box worked its way into our blood because the family has been full of musicians ever since. You included. You could say that box and song are sort of an heirloom... although the box itself is long gone. Still, they offer a promise that hope will find you, no matter the circumstances."

When she says these words, chills run up my arms. I find it uncanny I was so attracted to this music box from the start, but now I'm beginning to wonder if I was meant to find it, to learn more. Though I'm not quite sure if the music box was meant to find me, or if *I* was meant to find the music box...

"Alice? Are you still there?"

I realize I've been contemplating all this in silence.

"Mom, you're never going to believe this, but something really unexpected has happened."

"Go on..." I hear keys jangling on the other side of the line.

"I found the music box inside that pile of items you asked me to bring to Harper for the store."

Now it's my mother's turn to go silent. After a long hesitation, she asks—"*The* music box? Are you sure it's the same one? I can't imagine how it got in there..."

"I even found a note inside." I nod my head, determination rising. "Mom, I'm going to find this side of the family."

She sighs. "Sweetheart, I hate to break it to you, but I don't know if any of them are still living. My grandmother passed, and the rest of them would be so old by now..."

Her words offer a cold splash of reality to my cozy fantasy of a family reunion. But even still... "I have to try."

"I love you for that."

I smile. "I love you too."

We exchange have-a-good-day pleasantries before hanging up, and I tiptoe back inside, music box in hand. With this now resolved, I wonder if I can get a couple hours of sleep before the rest of the house wakes up...

Several hours later, I am seated in the passenger seat of Sullivan's Camry, a box of Callie's Hot Little Biscuits in my lap and two iced teas in the cupholders.

I take a sip of my tea, perfectly sweetened, then enjoy one of the buttermilk biscuits Callie's is famous for baking to perfection.

Nobody makes biscuits like Callie's. If I lived in Charleston, I'd make a point to get these biscuits once a week... and even that, I suspect, would not feel like enough.

As Sullivan slows to a stop at a red light, I pass him the biscuit box, and he pulls out a biscuit that's cheddar and chive flavored. Then he glances toward me. "I love that you're so excited about this, Alice."

I smile at him, taking the box back and secretly hoping he doesn't try to snatch one of the buttermilks.

Sullivan bites down on his bottom lip and prepares to turn right. "I have to admit—I am just the slightest bit concerned where all this may lead."

I hold up my hands. "Fear not... I understand my life is not a made-for-television Christmas movie. Actually, I talked with my mom this morning on the phone, and she prepared me that the story may have a sad ending."

Sullivan raises his eyebrows in question as he keeps his attention on the cobblestone streets.

"Apparently the music box once belonged to someone who never returned from war."

"That *is* sad," Sullivan says.

"Well, there's more. Get this—my mom said the box was a gift to my great-grandmother. Or was it my great, great-grandmother? I don't remember... the point is... I'm related to them. Maybe."

Sullivan slowly nods. "So that's why you're intent on learning more."

I hadn't been willing to admit this to myself until I hear him say the words. But he's absolutely right. That's exactly why I need to learn more.

See, my mother went missing during Hurricane Katrina, and I lived a very long time not knowing whether she was gone.

Though I found her—with some help from Sullivan—and we have begun to heal from the pain of that separation, I find I still ache sometimes.

Like how a formerly-broken bone is the first thing to hurt when you develop a fever. Those weak spots, in body and mind and heart, are simply different after fracture. At least, in my case.

And so, yes—I do crave a sense of belonging, of information about my extended family. Because for so long, my family was just my aunt and I.

I adored her then, and I adore her still... but I've always longed to know the stories of the silent. The stories of those who've gone before.

And this box in my hands?

Maybe—despite all the uncertainty in my life right now —it can give me some answers.

Maybe if I learn more about where I came from, I can figure out where I'm going.

Sullivan pulls to a stop on the street outside a charming "single house" in historic Charleston. I take the last slurp

CHRISTMAS ON KING STREET   23

from my sweet tea, and set the now-empty box of biscuits down on the floorboard before looking at him.

Sullivan reaches for my hand. "No matter what happens, I love you, Alice."

I can't help but grin. His fingers are warm and comforting against my own. "I love you back."

I look through the window toward the house. "What do you think we'll find in there?"

He shrugs. "Only one way to find out."

Before I can open my car door, Sullivan hustles over to open it for me. His gentlemanly manners do not go unnoticed.

"Thank you." I step out, the music box carefully cradled under my arm, and Sullivan and I walk hand-in-hand toward the front door.

I am a bundle of nerves and suddenly panic as the reality of what we're doing sets in. Was this a good idea?

Before I have a chance to voice my concern to Sullivan, a woman appears from the side of the house. She holds gardening tools and welcomes us with a warm smile.

"How may I help y'all?" She asks the question in a deeply-Charlestonian drawl.

"I'm Alice, and this is my boyfriend Sullivan."

He waves on cue.

"We're here to see if you know anything about this heirloom we recently found." I hold out the music box.

She steps forward as I wind the box.

As the music begins to play, her eyes grow wide. She sets her gardening tools down on the grass and covers her heart with her hands.

And then she whispers, "Oh, my..."

FOUR

1942 - CHARLESTON, SC

KIT FORD SWIPED Elizabeth Arden red over her lips. Then she put the lipstick back into her envelope-style clutch and set it on the table.

With a pat of her hand to her pinned curls and a quick check that her faux diamonds fell perfectly in place against the sweetheart neckline of her cherry red dress, she took a deep breath.

She was ready to meet some men.

Her patriotic duty. Raising morale and whatnot.

Her sister Louise was always teasing Kit about being a flirt with the soldiers, and it'd become a bit of a running joke between them.

But on some level, Kit knew—in a way Louise could never understand—that flattering a soldier gave him something to dream about out on the warfront. A reason to come home.

Maybe not a dream of *Kit* herself—but for what she represented. For a life built with a lovely girl who wanted to settle down and have a child or two or twelve.

And all these things, all these dreams, could make a difference when soldiers were so far from the comforts of home and feeling ready to give up. She knew it because a couple of them had written her letters from Europe and told her as much.

She was proud of the way she'd made herself useful to the war effort, in addition to organizing victory gardens and food drives.

It was one thing she'd accomplished that had actually gained the approval of her very buttoned-up father.

Okay, so maybe not the flirting part... though that truly was harmless... but he approved of everything else. Which was saying something, because usually Kit's impulsive ways brought little more than a sigh from his lips.

But she couldn't help it. Even as a child, she'd been drawn to things that were fun. Kit had never understood why that was such a problem.

So what if she didn't like sitting still as a kid or would rather paint a fence than a canvas? Her teachers seemed so taken aback by her natural curiosity.

Yes, they may have called her personality *trouble-making*, but she preferred to call it *charisma*.

And the soldiers seemed to agree.

For once, silly as it may sound, Kit had a sense of purpose.

So when the band leader announced a swing circle, Kit was quick to weave her way through the gathering crowd on the dance floor. Unlike many of her girlfriends, she relished the attention of the spotlight.

The band began to play a Lindy Hop tune as Kit took a brave step into the middle of the circle—typically one would do this with a partner, but Kit was willing to bet someone would step up soon enough.

And at the very same time she took that first step, a man walked into the circle from the other side.

He was... well, *very* handsome, there's no other way to put it, and he wore his winsome grin with the same ease he wore his uniform.

With his dark hair parted sharply to the side and his hand outstretched, he stepped closer still, and Kit took his hand gladly.

She met his gaze, and something unexpected passed between them. She felt strangely as though she knew him. Oddly comfortable—at home, even, holding this stranger's hand.

And a flutter of butterflies arose in her stomach as he slipped his other hand behind her shoulder and she tested out the security of his dancing frame.

She quickly determined this was not his first time dancing the Lindy Hop, for he knew just how to hold a woman so she wouldn't sling across the dance floor.

She liked him. Actually, she *really* liked him. And after a few measures of the basic step—of both Kit and the soldier silently testing out one another's abilities—the soldier raised a mischievous eyebrow.

Kit returned the gesture with her own sly smile, taking his cue as the two of them spontaneously broke into full-fledged Lindy Hop.

She leaned her weight into his frame, trusting his arm around her back to keep her nicely held.

The cheering crowd began to blur as Kit swooshed her hips and flipped her hair with every pass under the man's arm.

The man offered his arm in an L-position, and knowing the lead, Kit hooked her knee into the crook of his elbow, leaning backwards to touch the ground with her free hand.

This fancy dip sent the rambunctious crowd into a roar, and Kit found herself laughing as the man pulled her into position for the Charleston.

Legs kicking and arms twirling, Kit and the soldier danced in tandem as though engaged in an easy conversation—each bringing their own flair to the dance in the most complimentary fashion.

And then another man tapped her soldier on the shoulder—a common move for a swing circle—and before she knew it, her partner was offering one more charming grin before slipping back into the crowd.

She wanted to run after him, to ask his name and where he was from. Frankly, she'd never met someone would could keep up with her before.

But this other man was waiting, and the whole circle was watching, and she couldn't very well humiliate him.

So she pasted on her polite smile and determined to find the soldier when this forgettable dance was over.

She could only hope he'd stick around.

James made himself comfortable at one of the tables near the dance floor, a wide grin on his face as he thought about the beautiful woman he'd just led through the Lindy Hop.

"Why are you smiling like that?" His buddy George asked.

"Smiling like what?"

"Like a fool, that's what."

James had half a mind to smack him upside the head. "What'd'ya mean, smiling like a fool? Can't a man have a good time before he flies off to Europe?"

George took a glance toward the dance floor. "If *having a good time* is what you want to call it..."

"Okay, you want to know the truth?" James shot his own glance toward the swing circle, where the woman now danced a pedestrian basic step with another soldier. Should he feel guilty for his relief that the next man in line was a poor dancer?

James leaned his elbows against the tablecloth. "I think I just met my future wife."

Having taken a swig from his cup, George spewed the beverage out into the air. "I'm sorry... did you just say *that* woman is going to be your wife?"

James shrugged. "Why not? She's the loveliest girl I've ever seen—but more than that, we had some kind of connection." He shook his head. "It's hard to explain. But I guess you could say going to war gives a man clarity about what he wants when he comes home."

"And what you want is the dancer," ever-predictable George said. Oh, he meant well, and his dependability was admirable, but sometimes James worried his buddy needed a little more zest in his life.

"Yes, and I need you to make me a promise." He said this part in jest, but he hoped—in his wildest dreams—he really may have a future with her. "When I marry her, if anything happens to me, I need you to take care of her. You understand?"

"Let me get this straight." George's eyes widened with mirth. He clearly thought this scenario as likely as teleportation. "After you marry the dancer, you're planning on dying, and you think she's going to want to marry *me* as a replacement?" George was often selling himself short, but the truth was though he may be shy, plenty of ladies took a fancy to him.

"That's right." James gestured with his hand as though rewinding through George's words. "Well, except for the planning on dying part—but you know, a man needs a contingency plan."

George nearly snorted. "Sure, buddy. I'd be happy to marry the beautiful dancer for you. It's the least I could do."

James tapped the tabletop then stood. "Great. Well now that we have practical matters resolved, I think it's time I introduce myself, don't you?" He stretched his neck to get a better look at her and realized she was no longer in the swing circle.

That did present a problem...

But he would find her. Whatever it took.

"What do you think you're doing?" Louise said in exasperation. Bless her heart—it was clear she really meant the question.

"What does it look like? Enjoying myself. Is that a crime?" Kit teased.

Her sister sighed, delicately tucking several strands of hair back into her coif. "Must you make such a spectacle while doing it?"

Kit shrugged. "That's kind of the point, isn't it? Of a swing circle at least."

"Father would be horrified if he saw—"

"—But father isn't here, is he?" Kit straightened the hem of her red skirt as she and her sister took a seat at a table near the dance floor. She hesitated to concede this "dancing break"—as Louise called it—but she really did need some water after her number with that dashing soldier.

"Who was that first man you danced with? You seemed to know one another."

At the mention of him, the butterflies started back up in Kit's stomach all over again. "Did I?"

"Yes. Did you meet him in the victory garden or your other war work?"

Kit hesitated, scanning her brain for an answer to this question that would allow her to evade the truth without actually lying. She came up with nothing.

"Actually... we just met."

Her sister's eyes widened. "You danced like that with someone you just met?"

"You act as though I accepted a marriage proposal!" *Not that I wouldn't accept a marriage proposal, coming from him...*

"Truly, Kit, have you no sense of decorum? Why, I thought you were long-lost friends."

They were long-lost something, all right. Soulmates, perhaps?

Kit leaned forward against the table, and she knew her eyes were sparkling because everything about her seemed so suddenly and wholly alive. "What would you say if I told you I think he's perfect? You know, for going steady. Maybe more. Maybe... marriage."

Louise looked back at her sister, her facial features void of expression.

"I should've known you'd scoff at the thought! Can't a girl have a little fancy once in a while, what with all the suffering and terrible things in the world?"

Before Louise could answer, inevitably giving Kit a litany of reasons why *fancy* should give way to logic, the shadow of a tall figure appeared... and yet instead of darkening the table, his outline seemed to bring fresh light.

Kit turned to slowly take in the sight of him. Her heart leapt, then began to beat rapidly in anticipation. And for once, she was absolutely speechless.

When they first met earlier, she'd noticed his appearance. But now, having danced with him, she noticed his presence—his confidence and allure. And all she could think was how badly she wanted to make a good impression.

"Ma'am," he dipped his chin.

"Sir?" She replied in like interest. She expected a rehearsed line, like, *"We didn't have the pleasure of formally meeting earlier..."* or even, *"I've been working up the courage to speak with you..."* Both of which she had heard before from very sweet but dull dance partners.

But instead, this man simply said, "I'm James," as though he knew he nothing else need be added.

"And I'm Kit."

It was when he took her hand in his own—gently skirting his thumb along her palm—that attraction began to build a deeper interest. And she liked it... very much.

FIVE

AS JAMES casually took a seat next to the sisters, Kit cringed, knowing full well Louise was about to test him.

Kit loved her sister, but the woman was more practical than a can of tomato juice.

Candlelight flickered from the Christmas-themed floral arrangement at the center of the table, even as the band kicked up a holiday Frank Sinatra tune.

Kit wished she was *dancing* with James to the song, rather than sitting here like a bump on a log, but she knew if she had any chance of forming a real relationship with the soldier, she had better play nice with Louise. Because Louise was the one who'd report back to their father, and their father had scared many a suitor away from Kit.

So here she was. And here she'd stay.

"James." Louise wasted no time. "Do tell us about yourself. You're in uniform, so we know you're a solider, and you're clearly as skilled a dancer as my sister. What else should we know about you?"

Kit averted her gaze away from Louise and mouthed, "I'm sorry" for James's eyes only.

His response—a lopsided grin—charmed her beyond what any words could. He regarded Louise respectfully. "Suppose you could say I'm just an average guy, really. Before the war, I worked for my father's insurance business. Can't say it was my heart's deepest desire or anything—I'm not particularly passionate about insurance—but it paid the bills and helped out my family."

He sighed, rubbing his palm with his thumb. He seemed lost in the memory of simpler times. Kit understood that feeling well, and the sacrifices she'd made for the war effort were so minuscule compared to what his life must be like as a solider.

James puffed out a deep breath, stretching his arm over the back of Kit's chair as if it were the most natural gesture in the world. Kit could get used to this.

"When America entered the warfront, I fought a nagging sense of responsibility for a few months. My mother was terrified and begged me not to enlist. But my buddies were all signing up, and I got word you're more likely to be put on the front lines if you wait for the draft. I'm not sure if that's true or not, but I didn't want to find out, so I took things into my own hands and enlisted."

He bobbed his head to the right, then left, as though considering his next words. "I'll be honest. I'm a little scared what might happen over there. You hear all kinds of stuff. But I knew if I *didn't* go, if I didn't do what was right, I'd never be able to live with myself." James shrugged. "So here I am."

Louise studied him a long moment. She must have decided he wasn't so bad—especially after his line about civic responsibility—because her expression softened, and gradually, a smile even appeared.

"Thank you for your sacrifice," she said.

"It's an honor." He took his time with the words, clearly meaning them.

"You know what?" Louise reached for the cardigan she'd draped over the back of her chair, then took hold of her purse. "Suddenly, I'm not feeling so well."

Kit's attention darted toward her sister, who, one minute ago, was completely fine.

"Could I walk the two of you home?" James offered.

But Louise waved the sentiment away. "No, no—it's still light out, and the two of you ought to enjoy the rest of the evening. I think some solitude and exercise will do me good."

James bit down on his bottom lip, clearly cognizant of the unspoken message Louise was sending. He stood, shaking Louise's hand before she walked away, and reiterating his pleasure at meeting her.

"The pleasure is all mine, James. Do take care of my sister, would you?"

"I promise." The way the two of them looked at each other in that moment made Kit wonder what exactly Louise was implying.

With a nod that seemed to seal the sentiment, Louise waved her goodbye, leaving Kit and James alone.

"I like her," James held out his hand to lead Kit back to the dance floor.

"The feeling was apparently mutual. And I have to admit, my sister does not like just anyone."

James's laugh was deep and warm, like a drink of hot chocolate on a cold winter day. "Unfortunately," he said with a charming grin. "Louise is not the sister I was hoping to impress."

Kit swatted his arm. "You're a troublemaker, aren't you?"

James shrugged, slipping his arm around her back as they began the dance. "You tell me."

Kit shook her head, grinning all the while. "You really want to know? Because I think behind the charming talk is a solidly-good guy of whom my sister approves."

"So, just to be clear—you're saying I'm charming?" His brown eyes twinkled.

Kit beamed back at him, following his lead in the dance. "Yes, James. I am saying you're charming."

"Well I have to say, that's an excellent first step."

As far as James was concerned, his evening with Kit was ending far too soon.

Their conversation had been so blissful that he hadn't found the right moment to tell her something very important...

He was leaving tomorrow for Europe. *This* was his last night before he knew war, and he didn't want to spend it with anyone other than her. A delightful stranger.

As the last song ended and volunteers began clearing empty cups and discarded napkins, James took Kit's hand and decided not to let go.

They wove through the crowd back to the table where she'd sat with her sister, and she retrieved her shawl and purse. James offered her his elbow and tried to freeze the image of her in that red dress into his mind—to keep him warm and full of hope in the days to come.

He didn't really want to think about the days to come. Not now, anyway. There'd be plenty of time for that later.

Tonight was Kit's. He would give her his full attention.

She accepted his elbow, smiling up at him. She was

stunning—any man would think so—but what he liked most about her was her feisty spirit and quick wit. And he imagined those two qualities would only get better with age.

The more time he spent with her tonight, the more thoughts like that he had... which was not his usual pattern at these shindigs. In fact, typically by the end of the night, he found himself tired and a bit bored.

But Kit had zest. She was fascinating and beautiful and endlessly interesting.

And she smelled like cinnamon candies.

The brisk winter wind blew as they stepped outside into downtown Charleston, and out of instinct, James tucked Kit a little closer.

"Which way are we headed?" He asked her.

"Queen Street."

"I was hoping it'd be further." He winked at her. "Say, Kit, what sort of girl are you?"

The two of them turned the corner, walking past rows of historic homes and cobblestone streets.

Kit stopped near a lamppost. She tugged at one of the pins in her hair, fixing part of her hairstyle that had loosened during their dancing. "Oh, I don't know. I guess I'd say I'm passionate but sometimes impulsive. I make a good impression, but when folks realize I'm stubborn they don't always want to stick around. But I do have a good heart." She shook her head. "You don't want to hear all this."

"On the contrary," James said. "This is exactly what I want to hear.

She grinned up at him from the crook of his arm. "My turn. If you could have one wish that comes true this Christmas, what would you choose?"

"Good question." James thought a moment. "A year ago, my answer would have been different. Something juvenile like an automobile. But now..." He met her gaze and sighed. "Now I would just like to know I'm coming home."

She didn't so much as blink looking back at him. And it was all he could do not to scoop her up into his arms and kiss her this very moment. But they were having an important conversation, and he couldn't very well interrupt it—that was something he'd regret.

"James?" She said, quietly.

"Yes, Kit?" He leaned down, slightly closer.

"I hope very much you come home too."

Her words warmed him from the inside out. "And what about you?" he asked, walking more slowly now. "What is your wish?"

Her smile glowed in the light of the street lamps. She needed no time to consider her answer. "When I was a little girl, I would wait until I knew my sister was fast asleep, then sneak out of our room and out of the house, into the garden."

"You were never caught?" James was humored by the thought of little Kit lurking around the moonlit garden blooms, and wondered if her mother ever watched from a window above.

"I was very sly." Her grin grew wider. "I was also very bad at falling asleep, so the rest of my family was exhausted when I took my little garden strolls."

James laughed. What a charming memory for her.

"So I would look up at the sky, right? Then I would try to count the stars. And I remember thinking if I just concentrated hard enough, I could total them up, and my friends would be so impressed."

"Did you ever get close?"

"The sky seemed smaller then." Kit sparkled with recollection. "I felt so free. So alive. So very safe and yet full of adventure."

"And your wish is to feel that way once more?" James asked.

Kit shook her head. "No, not quite. My wish is to have a child of my own and to meet her outside."

The response gave James pause. She had surprised him with her depth of thought.

"I feel very confident you'll get your wish, Kit."

She looked innocently into his eyes. "And I feel confident you'll get yours as well."

Perhaps their wishes might come together.

"There's something I need to tell you." James and Kit approached her doorstep.

She turned to him, a feeling of concern constricting her chest. "Yes?"

"I waited all night..." He was stammering, which—if previous conversation was to be trusted—was unlike him. "I didn't mean to keep it from you. We were having such a good conversation, and I didn't want to ruin that."

"—James, what is it?" Kit blurted out. She regretted interrupting him, but she needed to know what was going on. Did he have some kind of secret?

"I leave tomorrow."

Her heart sank.

Of course she knew he was leaving at *some* point—why else would he be attending the USO dance?

But tomorrow? She tried not to groan.

"Tonight has been..." he hesitated, searching for the right word.

"Enchanting."

He nodded. "Yes. Enchanting. *You* have been enchant-ing. And I wish so much that we had more time."

Kit's mouth suddenly went dry. She was nervous. She felt the weight of making each moment count and hoped these would not be their last.

"Would you do me a favor?"James inched closer. His brown eyes were warm under the fiery flicker of the porch lights.

"Anything," Kit murmured. And she meant it. She was so smitten by this man, she'd consider a marriage proposal right here and now—throw caution to the wind.

"Write to me." James's words were simple yet oh-so-sweet. "While I'm away. *Wait* for me." He began to shake his head. "Listen, I know it's a lot to ask, but—"

Before he could finish the thought, Kit took him by the lapels and kissed him square on the mouth. His lips were soft and tasted like spearmint.

Suddenly shy, she began to pull back, but he wrapped his arm around her and drew her in. She melted into him, wishing those magical moments might last for hours.

Pulling away after a lingering moment, James grinned widely as he raked his hand through his hair. "So yes or no on the letters?"

Kit rolled her eyes. "You're impossible."

"And yet apparently also charming." He slid his hands into his pockets, raising his chin as he teased her.

Kit laughed. "All right. I'll give you that one."

"With any luck, I'll be back here next Christmas for good."

"I'll be wishing and praying each day," Kit said, feeling her cheeks warm despite the evening chill. That kiss really did a number on her, and her legs were wobbly noodles.

James gazed up into the night sky and Kit followed his lead, as a shooting star blazed overhead. Bewildered, the two of them looked at one another—both hoping their wishes might come true.

"The view of the stars from your house really is something, isn't it?" James said.

"I think perhaps it's the company."

With that, Kit leaned up on her tiptoes to kiss him one last time.

SIX

KIT STOOD at the window of her upstairs bedroom, holding back the curtain and watching as gentle snow began to fall—visible only by the moonlight at this midnight hour.

One month had passed since James asked to write her. One month... such a short period of time, really, and yet it felt like a lifetime ago.

She feared for his safety. She feared for his loyalty. She feared their too-good-to-be-true evening was, indeed, too good after all.

Had she let affection run away with her again? Had she imagined the admiration in his eyes? She wasn't so sure anymore.

She knew full well the speed of their courtship—if one could even call it that—would be unreasonable in normal times. Only one evening together...

But these were not normal times.

Each day that passed seem to bring news of another soldier who wasn't coming back. Those dreaded reports had not yet reached her immediate family. Rather, it was the boyfriends and sons of family friends who had been killed in recent months.

But the darkness of death and the heaviness of collective grief hung upon them all. So that even those who escaped its grasp felt the unmistakable anxiety that *next* time they might not be so lucky.

Kit never expected how draining or pervasive the trauma would be back on American soil. But she realized now she was naive to ever think that war only took place on the battlefield.

Kit drew the belt of her robe a little closer to her frame as she caught a chill. The aroma of her mother's cinnamon pull-apart bread wafted down the hall.

She had all the comforts of home here—and she truly was so grateful—but she couldn't seem to look away from the window.

She didn't want to miss any shooting stars.

James never knew all the places dirt could cover his body—but such was the nature of war. One could rarely wash it off.

He rubbed his temples with his hands, trying to put together words for Kit in what must have been the hundredth attempt at a letter.

Every time he started to write, he hesitated about what he should say. Though he'd only been in Europe a couple months, he had seen death and violence like nothing he'd ever imagined.

He wanted out. Everything within him wanted out—he was not a hero or the type of man to run toward a fire and douse it with water. He could see the ways his time here was changing him—hardening and traumatizing him—and yet he could go nowhere else.

But even still, he was proud to serve his country with these men. And James wondered if maybe all of them felt just like he did. If maybe all of them wished they might blink and wake up in their own bedrooms back at home, away from this nightmare.

His buddy George smacked James on the shoulder just as he started putting pen to paper.

"Writing a letter to your future wife?" George teased. He clearly hadn't forgotten the promise James tugged out of him at the dance back in Charleston.

"As a matter of fact, that's exactly what I'm doing."

"And how's the old dame doing?" George took a seat at the table beside James, the canvas tent shielding them for a few moments from the harsh weather and their otherwise-harsh reality.

James looked his buddy in the eyes for a long while before deciding to be honest. "I don't know."

George quirked an eyebrow.

"I haven't had the guts to actually write her."

George groaned, dramatically hitting his forehead with his palm. "You met the girl of your dreams and now you're wimping out? I know I gave you a hard time about saying you were going to marry her and all... but come on, man. By some kind of miracle, she actually seems to like you. Don't sabotage your chance with her."

James ran his tongue along his teeth, trying to find the right words. "But what if I come home... well, as a different man than I was before?"

George sighed. James knew he understood. "I get it, buddy, but maybe consider this: what if she loves you anyway?"

James shook his head and chuckled. "Maybe you'd make a better husband for her than I would."

"Let's not go that far." George stood from his chair. "You know I can't talk to beautiful women without breaking into a full sweat and stammering."

"In my experience, women don't mind stammering so long as you keep them interested."

"And when have you *ever* stammered around a woman?"

James grinned, holding up his hands in defeat. "All right, all right. I concede. But really, George, you oughta believe in yourself more. You have a lot to offer."

George shrugged. "Maybe someday, if I meet the kind of gal who puts my mind at ease. But that woman is definitely not Kit." He pointed toward James. "So you'd better get writing. I don't care what you say in that letter—tell her the time of day!—but it'll be ready to go out with the next post, you hear me?"

James saluted with two fingers toward his friend. "Noted." And he meant the words, because he knew George was right.

Kit deserved more than a smitten schoolboy who was terrified of rejection. It was high time for him to write the woman a proper letter.

My Dearest Kit... it began.

Kit found herself sitting alone, her elbows resting against the cloth tabletop at the USO dance despite what her mother had taught her about table manners.

A tall man with dusty blond hair and a smile that could light the day approached her, asking if he could take a seat.

Kit obliged, though her mind was elsewhere. She knew at some point she needed to move past James and the evening they'd shared—wasn't it only a few hours? And yet she held the memories so fondly, she couldn't imagine herself ever really forgetting them.

Then of course she feared for his safety... though he had only been on the warfront for a couple months, perhaps something terrible had happened. If that were the case, would she ever hear word or always simply wonder?

"I'm Stuart." The man held out his hand, and Kit accepted it warmly, telling him her name in return. The man did seem kind enough.

"I must apologize," she said. "For I may not be the most engaging company this evening."

"Everything all right?" Stuart asked.

"May I ask you something?" This man would know the answer as well as anyone, would he not?

"Why, certainly." He smiled at her again, and Kit imagined that six months ago, she would have been smitten by him.

"If you were headed to war and asked to write a woman you'd met at a dance such as this one, would that be a platitude? Or would you truly intend to write her?"

The man rubbed his lips together, considering her question. "That's a predicament, all right. I suppose my answer would simply be that if the woman in question is *you*, Kit, I assure you, your soldier will write in due time. There's no doubt in my mind. Sometimes letters get delayed in transit, you know?"

She felt as though she could breathe comfortably for the first time in days. His words provided relief, like shade on a too-sunny day. "Thank you. So much."

"Sure. And if he doesn't write you, I'll be next in line." He winked at her.

"If it's any consolation," she said, "you and I would've gotten along swimmingly before I met James."

Stuart tapped the table as he stood. "Actually, that is a consolation... thank you."

Kit laughed, and he walked away.

A moment later, her sister appeared. Louise's gaze followed the silhouette of the man as he approached the dancing space up front. "Who was *that*?" She asked.

"He's just as charming as he is handsome."

"Oh, really?" Louise teased as she sat down beside her sister. "Do I have a new brother-in-law?"

Kit chuckled. "No. He's still available... if you're so interested, maybe you should talk to him."

"Is that so?" Louise leaned back in surprise, sending one more glance over her shoulder toward the attractive man. "Are you sure?"

"Yes, I'm sure." Kit grinned. Seemed even her oh-so-practical sister had been smitten by Stuart's appeal. "You know how I feel about James." Her heart ached as though bruised at the mention of his name. She savored the word on her lips even as it brought the pain of his absence.

"About that..." Louise bit down on her bottom lip, reaching for her handbag from where she'd left it on the table. "There's something I haven't told you."

Kit frowned, confused.

Louise unsnapped the button closure of her velvet bag. She searched inside, then took a break to look up and meet Kit's eyes directly. "I probably should have mentioned it before the dance—I'm sorry—but I needed to know how serious your feelings were for him..."

"You're speaking gibberish. Come out with it, already," Kit said.

Louise exhaled, pulling something from her handbag. When Kit recognized the shape as an envelope, her heart began to gallop in expectation. She all but tore it from her sister's hands.

First, Kit scanned the address on the back, her fingers lingering over the look of her name in his script. Then, she gently tugged open the seal and pulled out the letter.

Before reading another word, she checked the signature to be sure. *Yours always, James*—it read.

Her attention was torn between the letter and her sister, with whom she was furious. "How could you keep this from me, even for a few hours? You knew how desperate I was to hear from him. Why Louise, I thought he might be dead!"

"As I said, I really am sorry, Kit." The lowering of Louise's chin begged for forgiveness. "You love these dances, and you've been so gloomy that I just wanted to see you light up again."

"I've been so gloomy because I'm in love with him!"

Louise's eyes widened.

"Okay, maybe not *in love* with him—but... something rather close."

"I'm in no position to judge." Louise covered Kit's hand with her own. "I'll leave you to your letter."

As Louise stood from the table, Kit was struck by the oddity of sitting alone and yet feeling, for the first time in weeks, as though she finally had her whole heart back together.

My Dear Kit,

First I must apologize that I've taken so long to write

you. I fear that by now, you've either forgotten our evening together or have assumed my disappearance.

The truth is, I have been enraptured by you—first with our dance, then every day since with the memory. Every time I put pen to paper to write you, I feared I could not do justice to either.

When I expressed this sentiment to my friend George, he swiftly reminded me that a woman like you ought not be left waiting.

So here I am, without much to say except that I miss you. I think of you every day. And—if I'm bold enough to say so— I hope you're thinking of me too.

Yours always,

James

Kit held the letter to her chest and breathed in, imagining the smell of him as though he were beside her.

He was living and breathing and missing her, too, and her heart swelled with hope. This letter was a better gift than any of the Christmas presents she'd received a few weeks prior.

But the sounds of the band and the whirl of the dancers all blurred around her when she noticed the postscript.

Her heart began to race as she read it... the one question that changed everything.

SEVEN

MODERN DAY- CHARLESTON, SC

SULLIVAN LOOKS as handsome as a magazine photo when he pushes his sweater sleeves up to his elbows and follows the owner of this single house onto her porch.

I am trying keep my admiration of her home and garden to a socially-acceptable level, lest she notice my true enthusiasm. But the truth is, her house is stunning. Even jaw dropping.

The structure, like most Charleston single houses, was built to make good use of the breeze—the long side of the house faces the neighbors rather than the street. And in a similar manner, the front door is actually situated along the porch that spans this skinny length.

She's leading us to it now, even as I breathe in the smell of her evergreen hanging wreaths.

I tug my coat a little tighter, cradling the music box with my other hand. The winter chill is stronger here than it was back in New Orleans, and I haven't yet acclimated.

Though the sight of my boyfriend in that green sweater is enough to warm me plenty.

"Right this way," the woman says.

I smile at him as the woman unlocks her entryway door. I can't help but feel we are on the threshold of stepping into something exciting.

But I never could have expected this. As her door swings open, an exquisite living space comes into view, complete with Christmas decor. A staircase splits the room —its railing lined with fresh holly—and I smell gingerbread cookies.

Basically, I could live here for the rest of my life. Very happily.

The room even has that old house smell—you know the one—it's similar to the fragrance of old books. The smell of adventures come and gone and starting anew.

"Please have a seat." She gestures toward the sofa. The upholstery looks fancy, and I hesitate to sit on it, but I take a cue from Sullivan who seems very comfortable here.

I always forget that his extended family lives in houses like these. I can't imagine growing up in these three and four-story homes.

"I've just now realized I never introduced myself," the woman says. "My name is Judy. I'm so anxious to hear how you've come across this music box and what you think it means."

Her words—*what you think it means*—strike a chord of concern within me. Shouldn't she already know what it means, if she has the answers we're seeking?

Disappointment muddies my expectations, and suddenly I find myself hesitant.

I put a smile on my face anyway, and reiterate it's nice to meet her. I thank her for welcoming us into her home and set the music box down on the coffee table so she can get a better look at it.

"You mentioned you recognize the music?" Sullivan

prompts her, resting one hand on my knee. I like that he does this. It's a subtle gesture, but one that reminds me I'm not alone.

I cover his hand with my own, and he squeezes my fingers gently. Our own little code.

"Do you recognize the box itself?" I ask, before she's had a chance to respond to Sullivan's question.

Judy holds the music box with care, her eyes sparkling in delight as though she's just been given a Christmas gift. "I *do* recognize the music. My mother used to sing the song to me when I was a little girl."

All I can do is blink.

Her mother sang this song too? But how could that be?

She winds the music box and listens to the tune as the little ballerina spins around and around. She seems—for a moment, at least—lost in a memory. And then she looks up, remembering Sullivan and I are here.

"To answer your other question, no. I haven't seen the music box before. Only heard of it."

"If you don't mind my asking, what exactly did you hear?" I ask her.

"Well, my mother is the one who told me about the box when I was little. She said it belonged to her sister, and that the two of them would put all their finest treasures inside it —dried flowers and fake pearl earrings and a few coins here and there. She loved the box dearly and had many happy childhood memories associated with it. But of course when her sister married and moved, she took the box with her."

"And your mother taught you the song," Sullivan surmises.

Judy nods, running her finger along the edge of the box yet barely touching it—as though some fairy dust might carry it away. "How did the two of you come across it?"

"That's a good question." I cross my legs at the ankles which is something I learned from watching *Princess Diaries* as a kid... though I'm having second thoughts right now whether Emily Post might've been a more reliable source for learning manners. "I found it inside a box of my mother's things. She was planning to donate them and didn't know the music box was there."

I shake my head before continuing. "If I hadn't discovered the music box as I was sorting through the items, it could have been a disaster."

"Indeed." Judy paled at the mere thought of it.

"Your address was on an empty envelope inside the music box. At first I thought it was a note, actually." I smooth the fabric of my jeans absentmindedly.

"I see..." She watches the ballerina once more as though memorizing the movement. "I apologize I can't offer more information about its history, but I sure am grateful I've had the opportunity to see it with my own eyes."

"Would you like me to take a photo of you with the box?" I offer, suddenly realizing the woman might have a hard time letting it go.

She begins to tear up, then reaches for a handkerchief from her pocket to dab the tears away. "That would be so kind. Thank you."

I take the photograph using her phone, thank her again, and then Sullivan and I are on our way.

Minutes later, I'm sitting in his car once more—with the music box in my lap and the view of her gorgeous home filling my window.

I'm glad for the conversation and certainly enjoyed meeting Judy, but I can't help the disappointment filling my heart.

I pick up my tea, jabbing the straw around the melting

ice and hoping to get one or two more sips from the cup. My throat feels dry, and I find myself wishing I had more.

Sullivan reaches his hand over the back of my chair as he shifts his car into reverse, then pulls back onto the road. "I'm sorry that conversation didn't go the way you were hoping."

I sigh. "Me too."

"Who knows? Maybe you'll still find the story. It could show up where you least expect it."

I let his encouragement still the rumbling in my soul—yet I can't help but wonder about all the other things in my life that I *also* don't have answers for. Like my relationship with Sullivan, and what I'm going to do with my floundering store.

And as we drive past festive homes, decorated with lights and garlands, it begins to snow. So I once again tug my coat a little closer. Even though I'm inside the car now, it's an old habit, I suppose.

I set the music box down on the kitchen table near Harper and Peter's back door and get to work sliding my feet from my now-snowy shoes.

Moments later, Peter's grandmother Millie comes around the corner. She looks Sullivan and I over, taking in the puddles we've left on the floor.

Sullivan must sense her disapproval as well, because he hurries to get paper towels and wipe up the melted snow.

"Thank you, sweetheart," Millie says. "I've got a store to run, and the last thing I need is a broken hip from slipping on the floor."

I can't tell if she's serious or kidding or maybe both.

Millie has always been larger than life in my eyes, and I get a little nervous around her.

She sets the electric kettle to boil and drops tea bags into three mugs without asking if Sullivan and I want tea. But strangely enough, she's chosen the Earl Grey we both enjoy, and I feel warmed before she ever even hands me a mug.

Millie makes herself comfortable at the table, so Sullivan and I follow suit. She takes several slow sips of her tea, and that's when she notices the music box.

"Well, my goodness..." Millie reaches for the heirloom.

My breath catches.

I don't know why I didn't think to ask her before.

"I haven't seen this thing in years. Kit's box, isn't it? Though technically it belonged to her daughter."

All at once, goosebumps appear on my arms. "Millie, you knew them?" But as soon as I say the words aloud, I realize the answer is obvious. *How* she knew them is the better question.

"Oh, Kit was a dear. Such fun to be around. She never met a stranger and always spoke her mind."

Sullivan chuckles. "Sounds familiar."

"Now, you better hush," Millie teases him, though if her grin is any indication, she revels in her reputation.

"All we know so far is that someone who disappeared during World War II gave the box to a little girl. Who I'm assuming was Kit's daughter." I pick up my mug of tea, then set it back down as I realize my hands are shaking.

"Really tragic that he died during the war," Sullivan adds.

Millie stills. Which is very unlike her. A slow grin brings one corner of her lips upward.

Sullivan notices. "What are you not saying, Millie?"

She sets the music box back down on the table.

"I'm just wondering why you think James is dead." She takes a long sip of her tea as though relishing the fact Sullivan and I are hanging on her every word.

"Because he is..." Isn't he?

"Then how come I played bridge with him last week?"

My eyes widen on their own accord as I look over at Sullivan. I try to make sense of what she's just said.

Sullivan's expression is one of amusement. He shakes his head. "You are full of surprises, aren't you, Millie?"

She wags her eyebrows, her smile widening. "I like to keep things interesting. Glad I could help out with this one."

She takes another dainty drink of her tea. "In the future, when you find yourself on a search for historical artifacts and their history, please don't forget that somebody around here actually lived it."

I chuckle to myself. "You're right, Millie. We should've come to you first."

She nods, clearly satisfied with this response. "Now that we've got that cleared up, who wants to take me ice skating?"

"Peter would kill me," Sullivan says.

Millie stands to rinse her mug at the sink. "Which is precisely why Peter will be spending the afternoon salvaging some old ironwork on Queen Street. A tip was called in about an hour ago... by yours truly."

"Millie!" Sullivan and I say in unison, though I can't help but admire the lengths to which she'll go for an adventure.

"I will take you on one condition," Sullivan tells her.

"Which is?"

"We go slow, and you hold on to my arm the entire time."

Millie shoots a mischievous glance toward me, and before she says anything, I know exactly what she's thinking.

"Sugar," she says to Sullivan, "The way that green sweater fits you, I'll hold your hand too if you just ask nicely."

I laugh to myself, not minding in the slightest bit that I've just become the third wheel to Peter's very charming grandmother.

I suspect that in reality, Millie will be the one keeping Sullivan from falling on the ice, rather than the other way around.

EIGHT

1943 - CHARLESTON, SC

THE SUMMER HUMIDITY had finally relented, giving way to cooler mornings and breezy afternoons. Kit strolled down King Street with her sister Louise.

They passed a soda shop on the corner of the street, and a pang hit Kit—a longing for the days before cocoa was rationed, among so many other things. When the war was finally over, she planned to feast on eggs and cheese and candies.

She knew that food rations were such a tiny sacrifice in comparison to the suffering that many others faced. And yet these rations were a reminder, just the same, that the world they knew *before* and the world they knew *now* were two different things.

Though the war may end, somewhere deep down, Kit knew that "before" world was gone forever.

Still, she had much to hope for. The corners of her lips pulled into a smile at the thought of James's first letter to her.

In the postscript, he had written that he planned to visit in a few months. His father needed major hip surgery, and

James had been granted permission to return to help his mother.

Five months, as it turned out, would become six, then seven—for October was now upon them and still no sight of James. His father's surgery had been postponed.

But he was finally set to arrive in a few weeks. Kit found the closer the calendar drew to his arrival, the slower time seemed to move. So she was grateful for this afternoon on the town with her sister and the welcome distraction it provided.

"Come on," Louise said, tugging Kit's sleeve. "Let's look inside this store."

Kit followed her sister through the door of a charming shop on King Street. After the Civil War, much of Charleston had been destroyed, but a group of artists and musicians and historians—women, mostly—began a movement to preserve what was left of the old structures. Kit was so glad they did.

She wondered if this war would also bring devastation to the city—talk of U-boats frightened her. She wanted the war to stay across the ocean. But in other ways, when she heard of the atrocities innocent people faced, she wanted to run into the conflict herself and make a difference. Strange how one could feel both things so strongly.

Kit forced her attention back to her sister, knowing that her what-if scenarios did little good in the real world, besides the prayers they inspired.

So instead, she focused on distraction.

Louise held up a strand of pearls. "These are lovely."

"Like a movie star." Kit smiled. Her fingers absentmindedly grazed the fabrics of blouses, though she paid little attention to what she touched.

Finding a row of dresses, Louise held one up for her

sister's perusal. They had been repurposing old dresses lately because of fabric rations.

When Kit noticed the silk fabric of the yellow gown, her jaw dropped. The dress may have been made out of real gold for what a luxury this silk was.

The shopkeeper approached Louise and Kit, crossing her arms over her own modest dress. "Isn't that something? We haven't been able to use silk in our designs since the war started, but we received this piece from another store. I knew it was a gem from the moment I saw it."

"Kit, this is perfect for you." Louise held it out toward her.

But Kit shook her head. Purchasing such a dress felt downright disgraceful when the world was in such upheaval. "Where would I wear it?"

"Isn't it obvious?" Louise ran one hand along the back of the dress, scooping up the extra fabric in her arm. "When James returns."

"Is James going to return as a prince?" Kit teased, and the shopkeeper chuckled.

"I'll leave you to it." Realizing she was not making a sale, the woman made her way back to the cash register.

"Come on, Kit," Louise urged. "Since when am I the adventurous one around here?"

Since I fell in love with a man fighting a war across the ocean.

Kit needn't say the words out loud, even though they were true. She suspected Louise already knew.

Writing James had changed her perspective on a lot of things—and she was no longer the carefree spirit who flirted with soldiers at USO dances.

Her eyes had been opened to something greater—in a blink, she'd matured from a girl to a woman. Now she read the papers to keep up with news on the warfront and had even applied to join the Red Cross.

She didn't want to simply *look* like she was contributing any longer. She wanted to really and truly contribute.

Kit didn't need the glitz and glamour of new men or pretty dresses. She'd found something real, and true, and lasting.

Like those vegetables shimmying up through the dirt of her victory gardens. The scrap drive she organized.

The patches on her skirts. The everyday spots that faded with wear but were no less valuable because of it.

And she had James to thank. Without him, she'd still be chasing the unattainable—but with him, she'd realized all she needed was already right here.

Kit took the gown from Louise's arms, gave it a once-over, and then placed it back on the rack.

The gown may be lovely, and the silk may be rare. A year ago, she would have bought it without hesitation.

But today, she would leave it for someone else to purchase.

November may traditionally bring the first chills of winter, but as James stepped off the aircraft back onto American soil, his heart burned with fiery anticipation.

He hugged his mama tight and pushed his daddy's wheelchair as the three of them made their way into the parking lot, then drove home from the airport. His mama kept crying and touching his arm like she did when she had too much emotion and no place to put it.

He'd never appreciated her warm hugs like he did now. But he'd be lying if he said he didn't feel some guilt and concern too—heaps of both, actually—for all the men he'd left behind.

He knew he'd be back on the warfront soon enough, but meanwhile, his subconscious still measured his days by drills and combat and mealtimes. He wondered if he would ever *stop* measuring his days by these things, for they'd become such a deep part of him, whether he liked that or not.

But for now, he had other things to think about—getting his father healthy, and seeing his girl Kit.

Her letters had been sunshine to him amidst the darkness of war. When he'd met her at the dance, he was immediately smitten—he'd liked her then, a lot.

But now he loved her.

And he couldn't wait to let her know.

James's mother turned from the front seat to take a good look at him. "I can't even tell you how grateful I am you're home. Even if it's for a little while."

He reached to pat her shoulder and smiled. "Thanks, Mama. You know I missed you and your cooking."

She laughed. Feeding people was her favorite way to take care of them, and James and his father benefited from that more than anybody.

"My surgery isn't until Friday—you going to see your sweetheart?" His father asked.

James raked his hand through his sharply-parted hair. "Yeah, I think I'll drive over tomorrow, if that's all right." He hesitated. Now seemed like a good time to bring this up... "Actually, I was planning on talking to her dad."

His mother squealed, knowing full well what conversation James intended to have. "Oh, James. I'm so delighted." She clasped her hands together. "He will love you—I'm sure of it."

"I hope so." James breathed in deeply, shaking his head. "Kit described him as pretty strict, so I don't really know what to expect."

"Just be yourself, Son." James's father said. "That's all you can do, and all you need."

James buttoned his coat jacket as he strolled the streets of Charleston. He wore a cap on his head and donned his very best loafers.

All around, the city seemed to hum with merriment as though joining in on a Christmas carol. Homes were trimmed with garland and poinsettias. Windows proudly showed trees with lights and ornaments, and James liked to imagine the houses all smelled like cinnamon and peppermint inside.

He turned the corner onto Queen Street and couldn't help but feel as though he'd stepped into a dream. A dream to which he belonged.

But as he neared Kit's house, his palms began to sweat as he mentally rehearsed what he would say to Kit's father. He had purposely chosen a time when Kit and Louise would be at their victory garden so that he and their father could speak openly, without expectation.

He took the walkway to their front door and drew in a deep breath as he reached out, knocking twice.

A man his father's age was quick to open the door, and he surprised James with his gentle expression and smile. From Kit's description, James had pictured her father as a harsh man... but that descriptor did not characterize the person before him.

Maybe war had changed James' perspective, or maybe

Kit had been such a spirited child that her father had no choice *but* to temper her enthusiasm.

Regardless, James held out his hand. He felt surprisingly comfortable already. But before he could introduce himself, the man stopped him.

"You must be James." His tone was even-keeled.

"Yes, sir." James removed his hat out of respect.

"I'm Frank." Kit's father watched him a long moment. James must've passed the inspection, because then the man said, "Why don't you come inside?"

James nodded, following gladly through the open door.

"I have to admit," Frank said. "Your visit is not entirely unexpected."

James felt his heart pick up its pace. He needed this conversation to go well. He *really* needed this conversation to go well.

"Why is that, sir?"

"Call me, Frank, would you?" The man settled into a sofa in their formal sitting room and motioned for James to take a seat. "I'll cut to the chase here. Kit has never stayed in a relationship longer than two months. She grows bored, and then she leaves 'em high and dry."

He crossed his ankle over his knee and leaned back, resting one arm over the sofa. "You're different."

James knew he was grinning like a fool, and he didn't even try to hide his smile. "With all due respect... Frank... she is different as well."

"She is that." The man chuckled, shaking his head. "That girl has always kept me on my toes. I suspect she'll provide her husband with an endless array of adventure." He put both feet back on the ground. "That is why you're here, I assume? To ask for her hand?"

James swallowed the knot in his throat. He hadn't

expected Frank to broach the subject quite so abruptly, but... "Yes."

"Good. Good." The second time he said the word, Frank punctuated it. "Look, I always thought when it came time to have this conversation, I'd want to scare the young man senseless. Kit's precious to me, and I won't give my blessing to just any old chap. But the thing is, I already know you, James... Kit's told me about your parents and your hobbies and your work ethic. Fighting at the warfront shows plenty of integrity and class in my book. But most of all, what you've done to Kit... well, it speaks for itself. I've never seen her like this. She's matured and grown into the best version of herself."

A family portrait hanging on the wall caught James's eye. In the photograph, Kit was laughing, and joy seemed to flow from her like sunbeams. He could not *wait* to see her again...

"Thank you so much for your blessing, Frank. Rest assured, I will take care of her... and the truth is, Kit's brought out the best in me as well. I look forward to becoming part of your family."

James meant it with all his heart.

The two men spent the next hour talking about scrap drives and gardening and automobiles. When it came time for James to leave, he firmly grasped Frank's hand and thanked him once more. Having his blessing would mean the world to Kit, and now he felt as though he could finally ask her the question that had kept him going every second of every day...

Whether she would like to find forever with him, under shooting stars.

NINE

KIT WRAPPED her warmest housecoat around her long nightgown and tiptoed through the hallway of her home, careful not to wake anyone.

Earlier today, her mother had hung Christmas wreaths with fresh garland and bells on all the doors. So Kit made sure she didn't announce her midnight escape with a grand ringing of bells.

She smiled as she slowly slid out the back door, closing it to keep the chill of the night out of the house.

She thought about James, and how one year ago she'd told him that she would sneak into her own backyard at night as a child.

For some reason, ever since James had begun to write her, Kit found herself wanting to recreate those nights. Maybe she wanted to find her childhood wonder once again. Maybe she wanted to remember life before the war.

Maybe she was looking for her shooting star.

Kit raised her face to the heavens as gentle snow began to fall.

"Make a wish," someone said from the moonlight.

Kit recognized the man's voice immediately as James. She had no hesitation, nor fear—she only wondered if she missed him so badly that she could now audibly hear him in her imagination.

But just to be sure, she turned around, and sure enough —there he was by the camellias.

She ran to him. She didn't care that she was wearing soft slippers in the snow. She didn't care that she had on a housecoat, or that her hair was in curlers.

She didn't know why he was here now, only that the moment was sweepingly romantic.

But she laughed as he twirled her through the air, then set her feet back on the ground below.

Her eyes adjusted to the darkness as James knelt down in the snowy grass.

Her raced raced, and her knees weakened. Because in that moment, suddenly she *did* know.

She knew what she'd never known before—the kind of love you ran toward at midnight, and the kind of love that ran back toward you.

"My dearest Kit," he began, his smile sparkling like the light of the moon. "There is nothing I want more than to marry you. You are my homecoming. My greatest wish come true. On my hardest days, you have given me a reason to keep going. The best moment of my life was the first dance I shared with you. Will you marry me?"

Kit couldn't believe this was happening—could not believe he was here. She wanted to reach out and touch him to be sure she wasn't dreaming. Her stomach leapt with the deepest happiness known to her.

James was home... at least for a while. And James wanted to get married.

She reached out and grabbed him by the shoulders,

pulling him closer—she just couldn't bear it any longer. "Yes," she said in his ear. "Of course I will marry you!"

James slipped both his hands to the base of her neck, gently kissing her. The tip of her head and the tips of her toes grew colder from the falling snow, and yet his kiss awakened a promise with her.

Then James scooped her up into his arms and spun her around, just as he had on the dance floor last year. And Kit closed her eyes, laughing all the while, memorizing every detail.

She knew she would return to this moment again and again. The night her beloved James proposed. A Christmas memory she'd cherish forever.

"About the wedding..." James looked into her eyes. "I'm here until Christmas to help care for my father, so I was thinking..." He bit down on his bottom lip in the most charming way, and Kit was so smitten, she'd marry him this very moment if he asked her.

"What are you suggesting?" She grinned back at him.

"How would you feel about going to the courthouse tomorrow?"

Kit had always envisioned a church wedding with family and a dessert reception afterward. A beautiful dress that looked downright royal in its many lacy layers.

And yet as she looked into James's eyes now, still in his arms—those old dreams became meaningless shadows. This man—this love—had lit her from within and was her true happily-ever-after.

So she looked deeper into his eyes and whispered, "I'd love nothing more."

And he kissed her once more, like a man getting married tomorrow.

The morning after her romantic midnight engagement, Kit flitted around her room, making preparations for the day ahead. Incredible to think that just yesterday, she was still dreaming of James's return. Now, he was her fiancé. For a few hours, at least.

Just went to show that from one sunrise to the next, anything was possible.

Two knocks on Kit's bedroom door interrupted her trail of thought, and Kit's mother and Louise stepped in. Both of them had erupted in squeals and hugs when she'd told her family the engagement news at the breakfast table.

It only took a moment for Kit to register that now, her mother was carrying a wedding dress.

Kit gasped. She had seen the dress in photos but never been allowed to touch it as a child because the dress was an heirloom... once belonging to her mother's mother.

She'd never even considered wearing it herself, though she'd long admired the delicate fabric and the feminine placement of the seams.

"I want you to have this." Kit's mom placed the gown in her arms, giving it a gentle pat for good measure. "Your marriage vows may be a tad hurried, but you still ought to feel like a princess."

Kit smiled warmly at her mother. "Mom, I really appreciate this... and the way you've supported James and I despite the whirlwind of events."

Her mother kissed Kit on the head. "Sweet girl, it may feel like a whirlwind to you, but I've known for months that you'd marry him. You've had a glow—and a grief—that only come with love."

"I brought you something too," Louise said, holding up a strand of pearls. She had inherited the necklace from their grandmother and had kept them safely stowed away in a jewelry box ever since. "I think you should wear them today."

Kit covered her heart with her hand. "But Louise, you've taken such care to be sure they remain pristine."

Louise nodded, extending the pearls toward her sister. "Yes, but this is a special occasion. Grandma would want you to wear them."

Of that, Kit was sure. She took the pearls from her dear sister. "Thank you. So much."

Louise moved closer so she could fasten the pearls at the nape of Kit's neck. "You're very welcome."

"Now, let me give you some marriage advice, and then we'll help you into the dress," Kit's mother said. Kit was all ears. Her parents' happy marriage had been one she'd long aspired to have herself.

"The good Lord has gifted you, Kit, in many ways, and you've got to stay close to Him if you want to know what to do with those gifts. There will be days you want to look to your husband, or to your children to find value. And those people are blessings. But they need you to show up day in and day out as the very best *Kit* you can be. Not what James says about you, or what your children do either. But what the Lord says. A good marriage is not effort split halfway down the middle. It's two people coming together, full in every way."

Her mother's words filled Kit's heart with admiration. "You are very wise, Mama."

"I am very experienced. Always continue learning, my love. In everything and in every way." She began unfastening the long row of buttons on the gown. "That's how we grow into the people we are meant to be. That's how we know what we're capable of becoming."

Kit wrapped her arms around her mother, giving her an impromptu squeeze. "I love you so much."

Her mom smiled softly. "I love you more," she said. "Now let's get you ready."

Before entering the courthouse, James led Kit by the hand to the sidewalk in front of St. Michael's.

"What I would do to have a photograph of you right here," he said. His words brought a smile to Kit's lips. She couldn't help herself for grinning like a fool. James had this effect on her.

Long, snowy white columns seemed to stretch from the church steps into heaven. Above the columns, a steeple housed the historic bell and clock that passersby used.

Melodically, the bell chimed twice, and James took Kit's other hand.

"Before we make our marriage official, I want to say this to you. When I promise you my life, I mean all my days. And when I promise to love you, I mean to cherish you. You, Kit, have changed me, challenged me, and charmed me. No matter what the future brings—no matter the upheaval in our world—I hope you never doubt what you mean to me, and how I adore you." James's eyes twinkled with each and every word.

Kit sighed. She wanted to swoon. What had she done to deserve a man like this? Why had God brought him to her, of all people? She was a confident woman, but James... James was in another class entirely.

Kit held on to every word. Her breath hitched as she considered what she wanted to say in return.

She tried to keep her hands from shaking as James held them in his own.

"James, when I was younger, I used to imagine what it'd feel like if I ever got married. In my dreams, my husband was always tall and handsome—"

James arrested her with his raised-brow expression, interrupting without saying a word.

Kit laughed at him. "And you are both of those things." Flutters of attraction filled her as she met his gaze.

"You are *very much* those things," she said. "But what I did not realize back then is how love goes deeper. That it's a choice on the hard days, and that it grows through the choosing. I never realized..." She inched closer, and James smiled at her, listening intently. "That I would *long* for the mundane after war, and that the everyday moments of breakfast and gardens, patched garments and coffee, would become my dream. Far more than any surface-level fantasy. James, not only are you my wish-come-true... but you have changed the way I dream. I promise you'll have my heart for now and always. Whatever *always* may mean."

"I love you," James said, and he drew her into his arms. His kiss was a whisper, his nearness, a hum—a chorus she wanted to sing for the rest of her life.

"I love you back," she said, and she meant it entirely.

Several hours later, after a dessert reception at Kit's parents' house, James told her he had a surprise.

He'd borrowed a buddy's automobile—a convertible, at that—and told her to pack an overnight bag.

Now, the two of them crossed the bridge to Edisto Island.

Much as Kit loved living in downtown Charleston with her family, something special lit the island of Edisto from the ground up. At sunrise and twilight, the sand seemed to glow with fairy dust—that was the only way to describe it. And anytime she visited the island, she wondered if she'd found Neverland.

This was a place where dreams and youth and nature intersected.

The vehicle rumbled down the road beneath sprawling oak limbs draped with Spanish moss. Then James pulled the car up to a small but charming beach house.

He turned off the ignition. "Well, what do you think?"

Kit stared back at him. All she could think right now was how she felt downright giddy to be his wife. She was really and truly his wife! She wondered how long it would take before that statement felt real.

"What do I think... of what?"

James laughed. "Of the beach house, of course!"

"It's charming, but why are we here?"

James's lips pulled into a lopsided grin. "I didn't think I would need to spell that part out, but..."

Kit swatted at him, laughing. "You should be ashamed of yourself!"

He ran his hand through his windswept hair with boyish charm. "I have a feeling you'll forgive me when I tell you that we're staying here tonight."

Kit's eyes widened. "Here. *Here?* As in... on the beach?"

"That's right." James beamed, clearly proud of himself for pulling this off at the eleventh hour. "One of my friends owns the place and rented it to me for a day. I thought you might want to walk along the beach, collect shells or sea glass, and watch the sunrise in the morning."

James met Kit's gaze, and his expression sobered as he reached for her hand. "Truth is, I wish I could give you so much more than this. A week in New York, or at least a few days in Savannah. But I hope we can still make this a memorable honeymoon."

Oh, it was going to be memorable, all right. Kit was sure of that—because James was more than she'd ever wanted, greater than she'd known to dream.

And even if they only had one day together in this beachfront cottage... watching the winter waves from the windows. Sitting beside the fireplace. Dreaming up new plans for the future. Even then, it would be enough for the rest of her life.

James tugged her carpetbag over his shoulder, and together, they walked inside.

TEN

SINCE THE ADDRESS Millie had given for James was located on Queen Street, Alice had insisted they stop by King Street for a short tour of the Christmas window displays. Then she asked if Sullivan wanted to get chocolates.

Sullivan was a smart man, so he knew the answer to that question was *yes*—whether or not he actually wanted to get chocolates was irrelevant.

After they were done with their dessert, they'd pay James a visit—and Sullivan hoped for Alice's sake that they'd find some answers to the music box mystery.

He reached for his wallet as Alice ordered their treats at Christophe Artisan Chocolatier. She turned toward him with the biggest grin on her face, and he loved that all it took to make her this happy was fine chocolate. Easy enough to sustain, as far as he was concerned.

Chocolates in hand, the two of them took the narrow staircase to the second floor of the charming chocolate shop.

Alice found a seat near the window, and Sullivan followed. She set two chocolates down on a napkin and gently pushed it toward him. "These are you for you. Earl Grey and raspberry."

"You know me well." Sullivan tapped his foot absentmindedly as they enjoyed their dessert. He looked toward Alice—her beautiful red hair was as bright as her spirit, and he noticed a crumb of chocolate on her face.

As he reached to brush it off with his thumb, she smiled at him. And he couldn't explain it, really, but sitting here with her in this chocolate shop at Christmastime made him see with striking clarity that he had everything he wanted in life already. With or without plans for his "next thing."

This was his next thing. Loving Alice, committing himself to her again and again every day.

He didn't need any more. And he didn't want any less.

So he knew he shouldn't wait any longer to tell her the truth. Because of his wounded pride, he'd held back from her, and that wasn't respectful or fair.

"Alice?" Sullivan said her name with hesitancy, and she met his gaze as she savored her chocolate.

"Why haven't you tried your Earl Grey one yet?" She asked, not registering his words.

"Alice," he tried again. "There's something I need to tell you."

She stilled this time, her eyes widening.

"Nothing's wrong. I promise." He should have started with that information so he wouldn't worry her. Sullivan drew in a deep breath, trying to gather his thoughts. He hadn't planned on having this conversation at this moment, and he wish he knew what to say. "You've probably noticed that I've been evasive when you've brought up the future of our relationship."

With one finger, Alice hooked her long curls behind her ears. "Go on," she said.

"You might have thought the problem is you. But it isn't." Sullivan shook his head. "Not by a long shot." He reached across the table to take her hands in his own, but she was holding a piece of chocolate. She quickly put it back in the box and reached out for him this time.

"How do I put this?" Sullivan's exhale was long and deep. "I guess I'll just be honest. I know that I was meant to make a difference at the hospital these last two years. I don't regret it—not for a moment. But Alice, the job changed me. The things I've seen... the experiences... I don't want to do it anymore."

"Oh." Slowly, she nodded her head as the information sank in. "Okay, I can see that for sure. I do wish you'd told me sooner..."

"I know." Sullivan fidgeted his hands. "I guess I had this idea in my head that it's my responsibility to have my life together. That anything less would let you down."

"But you *do* have your life together." She shrugged. "You're just... making a pivot, is all." Alice squeezed his hands. "Sullivan, I'm not looking for a man who already has all the answers. How dull. I *am* looking for a man who will let me help him find them."

Sullivan felt as though an immense weight had been lifted, and he could breathe again for the first time in such a long while. He should have given Alice more credit—he should have known she just wanted to partner with him.

"I'm really sorry for getting in my own head. *Of course* I want to have a future with you, Alice, and only you. I just grew afraid that I don't deserve you."

With that settled, she reached back into the box of chocolates. "Well, you probably don't, but that's okay." She winked to indicate she was teasing, though he suspected they both knew it was true.

"Sullivan, are you about to propose in a chocolate shop?"

"Would that be romantic?"

A slow grin slipped up her lips, and he felt a sudden desire to kiss her. "Actually, that would pretty much be a best case scenario for me," she said.

Sullivan laughed freely. "I've got something else up my sleeve."

"Suit yourself, but I don't know how you're going to beat handpainted chocolates."

Honestly, he didn't either.

I honest to goodness thought Sullivan was going to propose to me inside that chocolate shop.

For the record, I would've said yes—without hesitation.

Now, he bends to pick a wildflower that's growing from a crack in the sidewalk, then holds it out toward me. "For you," he says.

He knows I love these sorts of gestures... not only flowers, but also the fact he saved it from being trampled upon.

What is life, really, but a series of beautiful moments that seem tiny *in* the moment but so significant thereafter?

Perhaps this will be one of those.

I slide the flower behind my ear and kiss his cheek.

Now that we're outside once more, the winter temperatures chill me, and I wrap my hands around my arms to warm up. Sullivan notices and draws me closer.

I am ridiculously attracted to him and downright relieved that he finally opened up to me about his job.

But my heart races now because I know it's my turn to

tell the truth. "Sullivan?" I say, enjoying the warmth of his arm around me. I look up at him, meeting his gaze.

"Yes?" But his expression quickly sobers. "You look very serious. Are you okay?"

I nod. "The thing is... there's something I haven't told you either."

He stops walking just before we reach our turn, instead leading me toward a window display with an awning overhead. He waits patiently for me to continue.

"My store's in trouble."

"More trouble than last month?"

"*Much* more trouble than last month." I gulp. I haven't wanted to say the words out loud. I haven't even wanted to admit them silently. But I have to. I shake my head. "Sullivan, I think I'm going to have to sell the flower shop."

"Absolutely not." Immediately, he goes into planning mode, and I love him for it. "We'll host an event. A fundraiser, if we have to. Have you considered your social media presence? What about a newsletter list? A better website?"

I place my hands gently on his shoulders. Doesn't he know I've already considered all these things? And yet my heart is filled to the brim knowing he wants to fight for what matters most to me.

"Do you remember that scene in *You've Got Mail* where Meg Ryan's character does everything she can imagine to save her bookstore? She hosts author events and makes public relations moves, and I think they even picket."

"Honestly, I'm usually asleep by that point in the movie, but I feel like it's a bad time to admit that."

I roll my eyes at him, laughing. "My point is... after she has fought a good fight, she finally realizes something important. Her store mattered. Her store was beautiful. But her store *had* to close, and that's okay too. Because there was a next thing for her."

Sullivan looks back at me. "The question, my dear Alice, is what does *your* next thing look like?"

"I don't know yet," I answer honestly. "But I do have a hunch that the answer isn't *what*, but *where* and *with whom*. And maybe for that reason, the problem up until now has been that I've been trying to ask the wrong question."

"That's very insightful." He hesitates. "What does your aunt think?"

"She told me to sell the shop months ago, before we lose any more money." My heart quickens as my courage sets in. "What would you think about... maybe moving to Charleston?"

Sullivan's grin widens. "Funny you should say that, because I was planning to ask you the same thing."

I can't believe what I'm hearing. To say I'm relieved would be an understatement. I drop my hands from Sullivan's shoulders. "Let's talk about this more at dinner tonight, once we've had a chance to let it sink in. For now, let's find James."

"I think that's a good idea." Sullivan puts his arm around me once more, and together we walk down King Street.

As Sullivan and I turn the corner onto Queen Street and approach the doorstep, my excitement turns to worry.

What if James doesn't want to see us?

A million scenarios run through my mind, but Sullivan raises his hand to knock on the door before I have a chance to entertain the possibilities.

A handsome man with salt-and-pepper hair, a slim build, and a warm smile answers the door. Sullivan explains we are friends of Millie's and are here to see James.

"How wonderful. My name is Evan, by the way. I'm James's grandson. He'll be happy to meet you." He opens the door for us, inviting us inside. "Right this way."

We follow him through the living room, into a library where an elderly gentleman is seated. The man is wearing a WWII veteran ball cap and rests his hands on a cane as he stares down at puzzle pieces depicting New York City.

"May I introduce my grandfather, James?" Evan gestures toward him, and James begins to get up.

I'm quick to stop him, hurrying over and extending my hand instead. "We can come to you—looks like you're in the middle of something."

James smiles, communicating his unspoken thanks that I've given him permission to stay put but still retain his manners.

"I'm Alice, and this is my boyfriend Sullivan," I begin. I take a deep breath, wondering how he is going to respond. Is this wise? I hadn't considered the man's age before now—but looking at him, I hope the music box won't give him a shock. I never meant to upset anyone.

"It's a pleasure to meet you, Alice, and you certainly are a beauty, but I'm afraid you're a little young for me. That is why you came, right? Ladies can't resist a war hero..." The flicker in his eyes as he teases is not lost on me.

I laugh. "You caught me."

Sullivan just grins.

James reaches for another piece of his puzzle. "What can I do for y'all?"

"Millie gave us your address." I reach into my bag for

the music box, then begin to carefully shimmy it out. "I have something I think may belong to you."

James is slow in turning his attention away from his puzzle, but when he notices the music box in my hands, his eyes distinctly widen. He whistles low.

"Is that what I think it is?"

A slow smile grows on my lips. I can tell he recognizes the box by the way he leans slightly closer, by the way his hands begin to shake. And I feel both relief and anticipation knowing I'm about to find out the rest of the story.

Evan takes a seat across from us. "The box looks like an heirloom," he says. "Who did it belong to?"

"My grandmother—"

"My daughter—"

James and I give two very different answers in unison.

My heart begins to race as his answer sinks in, and I glance quickly toward Sullivan.

"I'm sorry—what did you say?" James asks me.

ELEVEN

1944 - EUROPE

OUTSIDE THE WINDOWS of the hotel lobby, the spring breeze sent leaves skipping down the sidewalk.

James sighed.

He was one of the fortunate ones. He'd been invited to participate in R&R, which consisted of a hotel stay, some good hearty food, and even better conversation.

Being friends with his superiors had its perks.

Now, he waited as a mail carrier reached into his mailbag and handed out letters and packages from home. James held his breath, hoping he would be among the recipients.

When the mail carrier called his name, James felt as though he could breathe again. He reached for the letter, quickly flipping it over to check for Kit's name.

Kit... his wife.

He grinned to himself.

He was a husband now. He had actually managed to marry the woman of his dreams—despite his buddy George's teasing.

Kit's interest in him made no sense. But he wasn't going to argue about it.

She was the moon in his darkness. She reflected all that was good about his life, his faith, and helped him to see the light once more.

Kit gave him hope for returning home. Hope for a better tomorrow.

James made his way to the street corner outside the hotel. He wanted to read Kit's letter without any nosey fellas peering over his shoulder. To keep anybody from taking his stuff, he carried his satchel with him and set it down on the sidewalk.

James read the letter to himself, wanting to slow down and savor the words but also in a hurry to take them all in.

My sweet James,

I miss you every moment—sometimes it feels as though I can't even breathe without missing you.

I think of our honeymoon on Edisto Island often. When I'm feeling anxious, I remember the sound of the waves. I pray God will bring you home soon, just as He tugs the tides.

I have some news that I hope will make you quite happy. I've fallen pregnant.

I know it's hard to believe, brief as our time together has been as man and wife, but sometimes things are simply meant to be for a certain place and time.

When I see a mother and child around town, I find myself wondering if our baby will be a boy or a girl. I am confident I will love him or her just the same either way.

You are going to be a father.

And I am finally getting my wish-upon-a-star.

Time for yours to come true now: stay safe and come home to me.

Yours always.

XOXO,

Kit

James held the letter close to his heart, but his trembling hands couldn't keep his grasp. The breeze sent the letter floating among the leaves down the sidewalk.

He raced after it, weaving through passersby and desperate to catch it before his wife's scripted words fell onto the street.

He retrieved the letter, just in the nick of time.

But only after he caught his breath and made his way back to his place on the sidewalk did he notice his satchel had been opened, and two suspicious men across the street were looking at him.

James frowned, crossing his arms as he looked at the music box he'd placed on his bed at the hotel.

He was puzzled. Why would someone leave this in his satchel? Had it been an accident? Did they mistake his satchel for their own?

Usually people wanted to take items *out* of other people's belongings, not put items *in* them...

Should he notify his superiors about the incident?

The faces of those men flashed through his mind's eye. Something did not sit right about them. Were they simply disapproving of a man who was clearly an American solider? Or did *they* have something to do with the music box?

Three firm knocks sounded on his hotel room door. When he answered, his commanding officer looked right, then left, before entering the room. Why was he so concerned with being watched?

"Are you alone?" The man asked.

"Yes, sir."

"Good. We need to make this quick." He walked toward the bed where James had placed the music box, then pointed toward the item. "Do you know what this is?"

James shook his head.

"Do you know who gave it to you?"

"No, sir." James had paid his satchel no mind as he'd chased after his letter from Kit along the sidewalk.

The man rubbed his eyes with his hands. "I don't know how to tell you this, James, but you've gotten yourself into a pickle."

"How's that, sir?" James's stomach sunk. The tone in his superior's voice was somber, even foreboding. "We have a high-ranking intelligence officer working to protect and recover cultural artifacts from the hands of the Nazis. The music box has been used for that purpose. But he was followed, and so he had to make an unscheduled drop outside the hotel."

James blinked, trying to make sense of what this man was saying. "What does all that have to do with my satchel?"

The man took a deep breath. "There's no other way to say it, James. You've been marked. Two Nazis identified you while you were on the sidewalk, and they presumably believe you are our agent. I watched the whole thing from the lobby, but I could not intervene without compromising the safety of everyone—you included."

"So..." James took a seat in the chair by the window, looking out over the world below—a world that now seemed so far. He could tell from the tight pull of the man's eyebrows that the next steps would not be what he'd planned for himself.

"We have no choice now." His superior shook his head. "We're going to need you to step fully into this persona. It's our only chance to keep our real agent active on the ground. We will keep you as safe as possible, but that means you'll going to need to come with us immediately. No goodbyes."

James swallowed hard, thinking of George and the other men whom he fought and toiled alongside. They would surely think him dead if he simply disappeared without any word.

But then he had another thought. Something far worse. He closed his eyes and tried to breathe, because he felt as though he'd been punched straight in the gut.

"May I communicate with loved ones back home?"

The man grimaced. "I'm afraid not. We can't risk a paper trail, or compromising believability."

"So you're asking me to allow my wife to believe I'm gone?"

The space between them seemed to grow in the quiet as the man hesitated to respond. "Your best bet to get back to your wife alive is to trust me on this one."

"How long will I need to carry on?" The weight of this new assignment was beginning to sink in as the shock subsided.

"I'd like to say it won't be long." He crossed his uniformed arms over his chest. "But the truth is, if the war continues, there's really no way to estimate."

As the man turned to leave the room, James threw a glance at the music box. "What about this thing?"

"Oh, you can keep it. Consider it a token of appreciation for your sacrifice." He reached for the door handle. "I'll be in touch later this evening with more information. Pack your bag and be ready to go."

James nodded. But the moment the man left the room, he fell to his knees and began to cry.

1945 - Charleston, SC

"Your assignment is complete."

James would never forget the rush of relief he'd felt at the sound of those words.

Now, as he stepped foot back on American soil, he couldn't help but remember the last time he'd come home for his father's hip surgery.

So much had happened in that time. On more than one occasion, he'd almost been caught by Nazi forces who still believed he was a government intelligence agent. Through careful monitoring by his superiors, however, both he and the agent were now home.

James patted his satchel for the hundredth time, making sure the music box was right where he'd placed it earlier.

He was going to surprise Kit. He planned to give the music box to their child as a gift. His heart pulled with both grief and joy, knowing the child was now a toddler. He'd missed the baby phase entirely... another sacrifice war had required.

He took a taxi from the airport to Kit's parents' house on Queen Street. He figured he'd start there, and if for some reason Kit had moved in the last year-and-a-half, her parents could tell him where to find her.

It wasn't until the taxi let him out in front of the house that James had a sinking feeling something wasn't right.

He couldn't explain it, but the house felt different than he remembered it. The reunion felt different than he'd imagined it too.

James approached the front door, but movement from a nearby window caught his eye. A little child... a little girl... laughed at her mother.

And her mother had an unmistakably round stomach.

Kit was pregnant.

James reached out his hands as though he might find a handrail to steady him—but instead he simply found empty space all around. He couldn't breathe. Couldn't swallow.

And that's when he spotted George.

His buddy, who'd made good on his promise to marry Kit if James didn't come back.

George kissed Kit on the side of her head, and she smiled up at him. And that's when James knew.

He could not break up their family.

He loved Kit far too much to do that.

So he pulled out a pen and a scrap of paper from his pocket. "A gift from James to his little girl," he wrote. He wanted to say so much more.

But instead, he set the music box down on the doorstep and prayed its song and his love would somehow echo for years to come.

For he had—indeed—come home.

TWELVE

MODERN DAY - CHARLESTON, SC

I'M STARING at James and wiping tears from my eyes as he tells us the story of the last time he saw the music box. Honestly, I'm trying not to ugly cry, but we're really approaching how I responded to *Free Willy* as a child.

"Is that how the story ends?" I manage to ask him, clearing my throat. "Was that moment on the wrong side of the window the last time you saw Kit?"

James looks at me with a mischievous grin. "Not hardly."

Relief does not even begin to describe how I feel when he says this. I glance at Sullivan, who is using his sleeves to dab at the moisture in his own eyes.

"But you left her with George to raise their child…" Sullivan starts.

James adjusts the brim of his veteran ball cap. "I did. I moved to Savannah so they wouldn't happen upon me in Charleston by accident, and George fulfilled his promise to me and to Kit until 1966. I saw his obituary in the paper, and I reached out to his father to pay my condolences."

"So after George passed, did you move back to Charleston and tell Kit what had happened?"

As happy as I am that James and Kit reunited, the story isn't making sense from my own side of the timeline. My mother seemed to think that James was really and truly gone.

And what *is* the truth, really? Could James be related to me? Which little child in the story was my own grandmother?

"Not immediately." James looks down, fidgeting his thumbs. Then he exhales. "It was a tough situation. I was still hung up on Kit—never did get remarried—but I also wanted to honor my buddy George and Kit herself. Didn't want to rush into anything out of selfishness."

I'm awed by his willingness to do what was best for his wife, even at the expense of his own happiness.

"The following year, my friend who owned that cottage on Edisto Island where Kit and I honeymooned put the place up for sale. So I placed a bid on it. Didn't want the house falling into the hands of just anyone. But turned out, somebody else wanted it too." His smile widened at the memory. "We got into a bidding war."

My heart warms hearing the lengths James went to secure the place he and Kit began their all-too-short marriage together.

"The two of us drove the price up so high that my real estate agent suggested I look into a neighboring property instead. But I insisted it had to be *this* house. And I won." He nods once, definitively.

"One month later, I was unpacking my boxes from a truck whenever I saw the figure of a woman standing on the beach at the edge of the property. She was trespassing, but just barely over my property line. I didn't think too much of it—figured maybe she was the other bidder or that the house meant something to her. She kept far enough away that she didn't seem to want any trouble, so I continued unloading the truck. Would you believe that woman stayed there all afternoon long?"

James picked up another piece from the puzzle he was working on. "Finally, as the sun began to set over the water, I got curious and went out there. I walked barefoot through the sand and sea oats. When I approached her, we locked eyes, and everything in the world stopped around us. The woman was Kit all along."

Chills run down my arms at the scene he describes. I imagine Kit's emotion, seeing the husband she thought was dead but who was actually alive and well. How jubilant she must have felt, being given another chance.

"She yelled my name—I'll never forget that—and ran to me. I ran to her as well, and swept her up in my arms, and spun her so fast that the sun seemed to set around *us*."

I look at Sullivan, and we share a smile.

James continues. "She kissed me, and it was the best kiss of my life. And then I told her everything. I explained how I'd been mistaken for an intelligence agent, how I had to avoid all contact for safety purposes. How I was the one who'd left our little girl the music box on the doorstep. She began to cry, so I took her hand, and together we walked home to the cottage. We lived happily together for a very long time."

I can no longer hold back my tears. To think that the love he and Kit shared overcame all those obstacles is remarkable. His commitment to her is inspiring.

I rest my hand on the music box. "If I may ask, what happened with Kit's children? Did they ever know the truth?"

James's expression clouds. "That part was hard. You see, sometimes war leaves consequences that trail through the years long after combat. Kit and I decided that since both the girls considered George their father, we would honor that. So my daughter and stepdaughter always knew me as their stepfather."

"I'm sure that was a very difficult situation for you." I mean the words. My mother's version of the music box's history is making a lot more sense now.

"You mentioned the music box belonged to your grandmother..." James begins, his eyes alight with hopeful questioning. "Are you sure of that?"

I nod, slowly smiling as my heart fills with happy memories. "Yes. My grandmother used to sing my mother the song, and my mother sang it to me when I was a child."

"Is that right?" James seems charmed by this idea. "Seems my music box became a sort of heirloom after all. But does that mean..."

"That I'm your great-granddaughter? Yes, I think it does." Impulsively, I lean over to hug him, and he hugs me back. He has no idea how much this moment means to me. How much I value my family's heritage after years spent trying to find my missing mother.

But he *does* know how happy I am to have found him, because I make sure of that.

"This is probably a lot for you to process." I set the music box down on the table beside his puzzle. "Why don't I leave the box here with you for now, and perhaps I could come back sometime this week so we can get better acquainted? I'll even bring donuts."

When James smiles back at me, I see flashes of a much younger man, and I imagine he was quite the charmer when Kit first met him. "I would like that very much." He gently pats my hand, not realizing he has given me the greatest Christmas gift I could imagine.

The next day, I'm a bundle of emotion as I go over yesterday's meeting with James in my mind.

I have a great-grandfather. I now have access to an entirely new family line of my heritage that I didn't know about before, all because of that music box.

And the man is a hero. I am proud to carry some of his DNA and only hope I can demonstrate half of his character in my own life.

Listening to him talk about his relationship with Kit gave me more clarity than ever how much I want to marry Sullivan. I realized, through their story, that circumstances in life come and go like the tides—and if you wait for everything to align... well, it may never happen. Just imagining how things could have been different for James and Kit had they not seized every opportunity makes me want to take leaps in my own life.

Leaps with Sullivan, yes... but also leaps with my job.

My aunt is right. Selling our flower shop is so bittersweet, but also necessary. I now have closure it's the right decision.

I need to move forward. We all need to move forward.

Such is my mindset whenever twilight falls over the city and Sullivan escorts me out the door for our date. I've changed into my corduroy skirt, a pair of tights, and my favorite cream sweater—which I've paired with the scarf Sullivan purchased for me in New Orleans on one of our first dates.

His gaze lingers on me sweetly as he takes my hand. "You're radiant."

I smile back at him. "You're charming." And *really* attractive. He wears the lightest brush of the cologne I like so much and seems even taller than usual tonight.

Maybe it's the way he carries himself—like he has an important space to fill. This gentle confidence won my heart quickly (albeit *after* our first meeting) and holds my interest still. Though I suspect Sullivan may age like George Clooney, it's his presence—his unspoken gravitas—that I find most alluring.

He continues to hold my hand as he leads me toward King Street. "I have a proposition for you."

My heart stops. Is he about to bring up our future? Surely he wouldn't propose on the middle of the sidewalk... though at this point, I would accept a proposal from him in an Uber during rush hour.

He continues, and I try to remember how to breathe. What will I say if he *does* propose? Should I jump into his arms like they do on television? Give him a kiss? Say something special?

"I know we both mentioned the possibility of leaving our jobs," he says. "And I also know in your heart of hearts, before you ever wanted to be a florist, you wanted to be a musician."

He is absolutely right about that. For a long time, my dream of music seemed too far gone. Too entrenched with disappointment and depression and trauma.

And it might have stayed that way, but for the grace of God...

Now, maybe for the first time in years, I can picture a version of my future where music plays a prominent role.

"What are you proposing?" The word slips off my

tongue before I can catch it, and the twinkle in Sullivan's eye tells me that my mistake is not lost on him.

"I thought maybe you and I could open our own event space where we host live music, and on weekdays, teach music classes. We'll keep it really classy—jazz and big band type of stuff."

"I like where this is headed." I squeeze his hand with both of my own. "I *really* like where this is headed."

"Good. Me too."" His grin widens, sending my heart racing. I can't believe I'm getting a dream-come-true with this man.

"Come with me." His step quickens, and I make an effort to keep up.

"Where are we going?"

But in response, he simply raises his eyebrows.

I laugh. "Can I at least have a hint?"

"Absolutely not. When I give you hints, you always end up spoiling the surprise."

"That's because you give terrible hints!" I tease.

"You are not helping your case here." His pace slows, and I realize we are stopping in front of Harper's building. But instead of going upstairs, Sullivan opens the door to the first floor.

"After you," he says, always a gentleman. When he turns on the light switch, I'm surprised to see strands upon strands of twinkle lights draped like stars. At the center of the room is a grand piano, with a bench large enough for two.

He doesn't need to say anything else—I know exactly where we're headed now.

Sullivan leads me to the piano bench, where I sit beside him as he begins to play. Hearing him play is a treat on any occasion, but on *this* occasion, it is nearly my undoing. I am a puddle of a person, emotion upon emotion, and I do my best to memorize all the little things about this moment because I know I'll want to return to them again and again.

First he plays the melody of the music box, which he has somehow learned without me knowing. Tears begin to form in the corners of my eyes.

But those tears fall with the next song—for this one has lyrics. Beautiful lyrics that are all blurring together until he gets to the chorus:

> *Alice, always and forever*
> *I promise I'll choose you.*
> *Let's run together through the flowers*
> *As they gently bloom*
> *And when the storms take the petals—*
> *Over and over, I'll choose you.*
>
> *Say you'll marry me and choose me too.*
> *Hand in hand, say 'I do.'*

He finishes the song with a flourish, then reaches into the pocket of his khakis for a tiny box. When he opens it, I'm met with the most sparkling, vintage-style engagement ring I have ever seen.

I am speechless. For the first time in my life, I cannot find a single word.

Sullivan simply grins at me. Apparently he's planned to say more. "Alice, I know things in our world are not necessarily how we planned them. I know leaving your flower shop is hard. But I *also* know there's a next thing for you. A next season. A next dream. A next pursuit. And as you step into it, I would be so very honored to come alongside you. To create my next thing too, until all our nexts for all our days join into something better than we could have imagined." He meets my gaze, and goosebumps run up and down my arms from the passion in his eyes. "Will you marry me?"

"Yes." I say it from the depths for me, as though I've never meant *yes* to anything before this moment. As though before, I was not capable of wanting and choosing and loving like I am right now with Sullivan.

A half grin appears at the corner of his lips. He reaches one hand just below my jawline and kisses me so gently that my head begins to spin.

"Yes," I repeat, and I kiss him again. "I will marry you, as long as you promise our business can be in this storefront because I want to sit at this same piano every day of my life —until my fingers are too stiff to play the keys."

"If that happens, I'll play them for you, and you can sing instead."

I offer a third kiss to his forehead, as though sealing our plan.

"Alice?" He brushes several stray stands of hair from my forehead. "I meant what I said. Our life may not always be grand. Some days may be downright mundane, or require us to change our plans. But I promise to be faithful and stand beside you wherever we go."

His words are a balm to my once-weary heart. And for all the romance of this present moment, what matters most is knowing that wherever we are—whatever we're doing— that will be enough.

Because at Christmas and all the days after, the music box has reminded me what really matters. Our people. Our heritage. Our hearts.

No matter what comes. The path may not look like we expected, but that doesn't mean it won't be wonderful.

I'm about to say as much to Sullivan when I'm startled by a clattering sound on the stairwell at the back of the store.

Sullivan shakes his head and laughs as though he already knows what's happened.

When I move my gaze toward the stairwell, I see Millie's head peeking out around the corner. "Don't mind me—I dropped my camera. Why they made the oldest person the photographer..."

"We made you the photographer because you insisted on it." I recognize Harper's voice even though I can't see her.

"Would you two stop it?" Peter calls out. "We don't even know if he's asked her yet."

"He definitely asked her," Millie says. "I can see them."

"And?" Harper asks.

"I think she said 'yes.'" Millie raises her voice to a yell. "Sweetheart, did you say 'yes'?"

I'm overtaken by giggles and the delight of knowing and loving these people.

Sullivan raises his eyebrows. "Ready for the afterparty upstairs?"

"I thought you'd never ask." I weave my fingers through his own, and together, we take the stairs one by one.

WHERE THE LAST ROSE BLOOMS

CHAPTER ONE

ALICE ALWAYS HAD LOVED FLOWERS.

There was something about the blend of colors, the hidden roots, the twisting petals as they unfurled in the sun one by one. A symbol of femininity—how that which is delicate can also be strong.

Whiskey in a teacup, as her aunt always said. Well, her aunt and Reese Witherspoon, but honestly, Aunt Charlotte had been saying that way back when Reese was still filming *Sweet Home Alabama.*

Alice swept petals from the floor, beautiful yet fragmented evidence of the fullness the day had brought. She'd been running The Prickly Rose, a customizable bouquet shop on Magazine Street, alongside her aunt for several years now, and Valentine's Day always left plenty of cast-off remnants.

She was sweeping the last of the petals into the dustpan when she heard a knock at the door. A quick glance at the clock confirmed they were a quarter past closing time, and if she didn't leave now, she would be late for her date.

Not that she was particularly excited about a blind

double date on Valentine's Day, but her friend Harper had insisted, so she'd acquiesced.

Still, it was the principle of the thing. No self-respecting person thought so little of his date that he'd buy flowers at closing time. Let alone fifteen minutes after.

Alice was just about to check the bolt on the door when her aunt buzzed past, placing a hand on each side of her own face to get a better look through the wrought iron. She glanced at Alice over her shoulder. "He's handsome."

Alice stepped down to open the trashcan, then dumped the petals. "They always are."

Aunt Charlotte turned to face her. "But this one looks like a young Clooney."

"I don't care if he looks like Milo Ventimiglia." Okay, that was an exaggeration. But her aunt probably didn't even know who Milo was, so she wasn't too concerned about the woman calling her bluff. Alice tapped one stubborn petal until it fell into the trash. "We're closed."

Aunt Charlotte hurried closer, glancing behind her as though he could hear them. "But the poor boy needs flowers. It's Valentine's Day, Alice. Couldn't you have a little heart?"

"I see what you did there with the pun." Alice planted her hands at the hips of her knee-length skirt. "But the answer is no. I cannot. He can abide by the store hours just like everyone else managed to."

"I didn't want to have to do this..." But before Aunt Charlotte could finish the words, she began racing toward the door.

Alice followed two steps behind but did manage to slam her hand on the door before her aunt could shimmy it open. "What are you, four years old?" she whispered. "He's probably seen us through the door."

"And whose fault is that, hmm?" Aunt Charlotte peeled Alice's hand from off the doorway.

Alice balked. "Why, I have never—"

But Aunt Charlotte was already busy opening the door. She smiled a warning sort of grin at Alice. "What if it *is* Clooney?" she whispered. Her eyes went wide.

"You think everyone is Clooney," Alice murmured as the man stepped inside. She managed a smile despite his tardiness because, after all, she was just the kind of person to be polite.

He took a step inside, and the bell at the front of the shop jingled.

Definitely not Milo, but—dare she say it—even more attractive.

He was tall and seemed even taller because of the way his presence filled the room. His smile revealed straight teeth, his jaw was strong but not sharp, and his shoulders, broad. He wore a relaxed T-shirt over properly fitting jeans, and faintly smelled of cedarwood.

He wore trendy tennis shoes that made him look ready to run... both literally *and* figuratively.

But despite his obvious appeal, he was a *customer*. And it was well past closing time. At this point, Alice was so exhausted that Clooney really could've walked into the shop, and she would've pointed to the *Closed* sign.

"How may I help you?"

One strand of the man's trimmed brown hair fell askew as he looked at her.

Their gazes locked, and Alice caught herself drawn in by a blend of curiosity and attraction. His eyes were the color of sea glass and the wild waves that made it strong.

Alice blinked, her mind foggy with the memory of waves.

After the slightest moment's pause, he pulled out his wallet. "I need some red roses."

Alice frowned. She looked at Aunt Charlotte, then back at the man.

"It's Valentine's Day," Alice said matter-of-factly.

He set his debit card on the counter and pushed it forward, as if the gesture would make a difference. "I am aware of that. Which is why I need them."

Her aunt smiled sweetly, ready to accommodate him, but Alice wouldn't be so easily swayed. She didn't like his bullying tone, and handed the card back to him.

"We're all out," Alice said.

The man rolled his eyes. "Fine. I'll take pink, then."

"Out of those too."

"White?"

Alice leaned forward, her elbows on the counter. "I'm sorry. Nope."

The man sighed as he looked straight into her eyes once more, clearly not used to hearing the word *no*. He pocketed his hands. "Let me put it this way. What *do* you have?"

Alice kneeled beneath the register and chose another arrangement to set up on the counter.

The man touched the whimsical array of baby's breath, berries, dried cotton, and pinecones as though it were a prickly cactus. He tapped the glass with his finger. "This is a mason jar."

Alice cleared her throat. "It's an antique. That's something we pride ourselves in here at The Prickly Rose—no two of our items are identical." She wouldn't mention the flowers were two days old and half-off because the petals had begun to droop. That's what he got for waiting until the last minute.

"This is stuff you could find in your backyard."

Had he heard *anything* she'd just said?

"It's organic." She swallowed to fight the tide in his eyes, hating the amount of willpower it took to do that.

"I cannot bring her a jar of berries and squirrel seeds. I'm trying to leave a good impression here."

I hope for your sake your impression on her is better than the one you've left on me.

"Sorry we can't be of greater help." Alice shrugged, thankful to soon be rid of him. Sometimes these after-store-hours customers could be equally insensitive to overstaying their welcome. "You've caught us after closing time, so it's pretty picked over."

He turned to the door with a wave over his shoulder. "Thanks anyway," he mumbled, on the very edge of rudeness.

But as the bell above the door chimed, Alice realized her aunt was smiling a dangerous sort of smile.

"Well, he was darling."

Alice rolled her eyes. Her aunt was convinced Alice's prospects for a suitable marriage expired after age twenty-nine. Which left her six months.

She shook her head and fiddled with the mason jar arrangement before placing it back under the counter. "Late for a date on Valentine's Day? Definitely not my type."

Obviously, Sullivan had made a mistake. Buying flowers for his blind date had resulted in unequivocal failure.

What was worse, a quick glance at his phone showed he was ten minutes late to meet his friends. And counting. He was lost. In the French Quarter. He had passed this nostalgia shop at least three times now and was walking in circles.

Maybe his date wouldn't be the flowers type.

Who was he kidding? All women were the flowers type. His mother had taught him that. And his Grandma Beth would disown him if she knew he was about to show up to a date on Valentine's Day empty-handed.

Sure, it wasn't a serious date or anything, but the woman was a friend of a friend and the day was really Valentine's Day, so he was pretty sure those two things combined qualified her for a bouquet.

A lot of help the woman at the flower shop had been. He had every intention of giving her a one-star review, but his phone lit up with the notification his buddy Peter was calling.

"Dude, where are you?"

Sullivan spun around to get a look at the street name. "I'm here... ish. I just can't seem to find the place."

"Okay, I'm going out into the street now to see if I can find you."

Suddenly, he saw Peter waving from one block up. Sullivan waved back and hustled over.

The two men clasped hands. "Sorry, man. I got turned around."

"It happens." Peter smiled. "Hey, it's good to see you. Been a while."

Sullivan raked his hair back into place with his hand. "Sure has. Engagement suits you, Peter. You look happy."

Peter's grin widened. "I am." Near the restaurant, two women lingered on the sidewalk. Sullivan assumed the woman next to Harper was his blind date for the evening. They were still too far away for him to get a good look at her.

Sullivan wasn't typically the type to go for the whole blind-date thing. But he, Peter, and Harper were in town for only a little while because of Peter and Harper's wedding in a few days. Harper apparently wanted to see this woman as much as Peter and Sullivan wanted to hang out together, so doubling up seemed like a good idea. They'd insisted he and his date would get along great.

And really, Sullivan didn't make a habit of turning women down. Well, not on a first date, at least.

It wasn't until he and Peter approached the restaurant that the nagging feeling in his chest began. Something about the woman standing beside Harper was familiar. . . . he had seen her before.

Then she turned, and he saw her face. Her beautiful, berry-squirrel-seed-loving smile. He rubbed his hands over his eyes. *You have got to be kidding me.*

Peter turned, the gesture not lost on him. "What is it? What's wrong?" he asked.

"It's just . . . well . . . Is *that* my date?" Sullivan nodded his head toward where the women stood.

"Yes, and I don't see why you're not falling on your knees in gratitude right now. She's totally your type."

Sullivan held up one finger and shook his hand. "Funny you should say that, actually . . ."

Peter crossed his arms. "What's going on?"

"I sort of met her earlier." Sullivan huffed. "You could say I didn't leave the best impression."

Peter hit him hard on the shoulder. "So here's your chance to make a better one."

Read Alice and Sullivan's
meet-cute
in Where the Last Rose Blooms

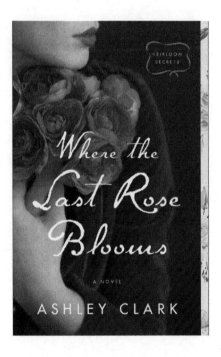

DEAR READER...

Thanks for taking this trip to Charleston with me! I hope you've enjoyed meeting Kit and James, and that you've had fun catching up with Alice and Sullivan too.

Things have been challenging in our world the last couple years, and it's my hope and prayer God renews your joy this holiday season. May your heart be filled with all the good things He has done, and like Alice, may you look with anticipation toward your *next* thing, whatever it may be.

Be sure to sign up for my newsletter to stay up to date! www.ashleyclarkbooks.com.

Until next time!
Ashley

ALSO BY ASHLEY CLARK

The Heirloom Secrets Series

The Dress Shop on King Street

Paint and Nectar

Where the Last Rose Blooms

The Heirloom Secrets Novellas

Christmas on King Street

Christmas at the Inn

A Valentine from Charleston

Made in the USA
Columbia, SC
12 January 2023

10052662R00065